THE TRA

"It *is* you," the earl sa..., own assumptions. Holding out his right hand, he advanced toward her, smiling widely. "Miss Quinton, I have to own it. Please perceive me standing before you, openmouthed with astonishment."

Immediately Victoria's back was up, for she was certain this smiling man was enjoying himself quite royally, pretending that she had overnight turned from a molting crow into an exotic, brilliantly plumed bird.

"Oh, do be quiet," she admonished, furious at feeling herself blushing as he continued to hold out his hand to her. "Now, if you have done amusing yourself at my expense, I suggest you take yourself off on your usual immoral pursuits, as I have more than enough on my plate without having to stand here listening to your ludicrous outpourings of astonishment."

Dropping his ignored hand to his side, Patrick merely smiled all the more as he unabashedly quipped, "Now you've gone and done it, Miss Quinton. Just as I was about to search out your uncle and thank him for having brought about a near miraculous transformation, you had to go and open your mouth."

Kasey Michaels is the *New York Times* and *USA Today* bestselling author of more than sixty books. She has won the Romance Writers of America RITA Award and the *Romantic Times* Career Achievement Award for her historical romances set in the Regency era, and also writes contemporary romances for Silhouette and Harlequin Books.

The Questioning
Miss Quinton

TORONTO • NEW YORK • LONDON
AMSTERDAM • PARIS • SYDNEY • HAMBURG
STOCKHOLM • ATHENS • TOKYO • MILAN • MADRID
PRAGUE • WARSAW • BUDAPEST • AUCKLAND

To Dorothea Sandbrook, librarian and friend,
who thirty years ago took the time to introduce a
restless teenager to the fascinating world of books—
and set off a love affair with the written word
that goes on and on

ISBN 0-373-51182-5

THE QUESTIONING MISS QUINTON

Copyright © 1987 by Kathie Seidick.

Visit us at www.eHarlequin.com

Printed in U.S.A.

PROLOGUE

"How COMPLETELY and utterly boring."

Victoria Quinton, feeling no better for having voiced her sentiments aloud, shifted her slim body slightly on the edge of the uncomfortable wooden chair that was situated to one side of the narrow, badly lit hallway, a thick stack of closely written papers lying forgotten in her lap as she waited for the summons that was so uncharacteristically late in coming this morning.

Raising one hand, she stifled a wide yawn, as she had been kept awake far into the night transcribing the Professor's latest additions to his epic book-in-progress on the history of upper-class English society; for besides acting as secretary, sounding board, and general dogsbody to him for as long as she could remember, Victoria also served as transcriptionist to the Professor, transforming his, at times, jumbled and confusing scribblings into legible final copies.

The Professor would not allow Victoria to recopy his notes into neat final copies during the daytime, and since her evenings were not known for their hours spent in any scintillating pursuit of pleasure, she could find no convincing reason to object to his directive that she fill them with more work.

As for the Professor, his lifelong struggle against insomnia made his evenings a prime time for visiting with the countless people he was always interviewing—all of them contenting themselves by prosing on long into the night over some obscure bit of family history of concern to, probably, none other than his subjects, another scholar, or himself.

Victoria had never been introduced to any of the Professor's nocturnal visitors, nor did she harbor any secret inclination to learn their identities, which the Professor guarded like some spoiled child hiding his treasured supply of tin soldiers from his mates. After all, if the Professor liked them, they would doubtless bore her to tears.

Hearing the ancient clock in the foyer groan, seem to collect itself, and then slowly chime ten times, she tentatively rose to her feet, torn between acknowledging that every minute that ticked by made it one minute less that she would be expected to sit in the gloomy library writing page after endless page of dictation until her fingers bent into painful cramps, and dreading the certain sharp scolding she would get for not rousing him when the Professor finally awakened on his own.

In the end, realizing that she wasn't exactly spending the interim in a mad indulgence of pleasure—seeing as how she had been sitting in the same spot like some stuffed owl ever since rising from the breakfast table—she made for the closed door and gave a short, barely audible knock.

There was no response. Victoria sighed and shook her head. "He's probably curled up atop his desk again, afraid that the trip upstairs to his bed would rob him of his drowsiness, and taking his rest where he can," she decided, knocking again, a little louder this time. Then she pressed her ear against the wood, thinking that the Professor's stentorian snores should be audible even through the thickness of the door.

Five minutes passed in just this unproductive way, and

Victoria chewed on her bottom lip, beginning to feel the first stirrings of apprehension. She looked about the hallway, wondering where Willie was and whether or not she should search out the housekeeper as a sort of reinforcement before daring to enter the library on her own.

But Willie was always entrenched in the kitchen at this time of the morning, industriously scrubbing the very bottom out of some inoffensive pot, or shining an innocent piece of brass to within an inch of its life. She had her routine, Wilhelmina Flint did, and Victoria was loath to interrupt it. Besides, Willie had a habit of overreacting, and Victoria didn't feel up to dealing with the possibility of having to dispense hartshorn or burnt feathers at this particular moment.

Also, the Professor might be sick, or injured in a fall from the small ladder he used to reach the uppermost shelves of his bookcases. What a pother that would create. For if the Professor was hard to deal with when healthy, as an invalid he would be downright unbearable!

Victoria gave herself a mental kick, realizing she was only delaying the inevitable. She had hesitated too long as it was; it was time she stopped hemming and hawing like some vaporish miss and acted. So thinking, Victoria straightened her thin shoulders, turned the knob, and pushed on the door.

The room thus revealed was in complete disorder, with papers and books strewn everywhere the eye could see—which wasn't far, as the Professor's huge, footed globe was lying tipped over onto its side, blocking the heavy door from opening to more than a wide crack.

"Willie will doubtless suffer an apoplexy," she joked feebly, wondering if she herself was going to faint. No, she reminded herself grimly, only pretty girls are allowed to fall into a swoon at the first sign of trouble. Plain girls are expected to thrust out their chins and bear up nobly under the strain. "Just one more reason to curse my wretched fate," she grumbled under her breath, pushing her spectacles back up onto the bridge of her nose, taking a deep breath, and resigning herself to the inevitable.

Putting a shoulder to the door, she pushed the globe completely aside with some difficulty and entered the library, blinking furiously behind her rimless spectacles as her eyes struggled to become accustomed to the gloom. The heavy blue velvet draperies were tightly closed and all the candles had long since burned down to their sockets.

"Oh, Lord, I don't think I'm going to like this," she whispered, trying hard not to turn on her heels and flee the scene posthaste like the craven coward she told herself she was. Victoria could feel her heart starting to beat quickly, painfully against her rib cage, and she mentally berated herself for not having had the foresight to have acted sooner.

"Pro—, er, Professor?" she ventured nervously, hating the tremor she could hear creeping into her voice. She then advanced, oh so slowly, edging toward the cold fireplace to pick up the poker, then holding it ahead of her as she inched her way across the room, her gaze darting this way and that as she moved toward the front of the massive oak desk.

The Professor wasn't behind the desk; he didn't appear to be anywhere. Lowering the poker an inch or two, Victoria walked gingerly round to the rear of the desk, as she had decided that the intruder—for what else could possibly have caused such a mess except a house-breaker?—was long gone.

She looked up at the ceiling thoughtfully, for the Professor's chamber was directly above the library, and wondered if he was still abed, and as yet unaware of the ransacking of his sacred workplace. "Wouldn't that just be my wretched luck? I most definitely don't relish being the one landed with the duty of enlightening him with this marvelous little tidbit of information," Victoria admitted, grimacing as she cast her eyes around the room one more time.

"Oh," she groaned then, realizing at last that the stained, crumpled papers that littered the floor at her feet constituted at least three months of her painstaking labor, now ruined past redemption. "The only, the absolute *only* single thing in this entire world that could possibly be worse than having to transcribe all those boring notes is having to do them twice!"

She flung the heavy poker in the general direction of the window embrasure in disgust, not caring in the slightest if her impetuous action caused more damage.

"Arrrgh!" The pain-filled moan emanated from the shallow window embrasure, and the startled Victoria involuntarily leaped nearly a foot off the floor in surprise before she could race to throw back the draperies, revealing the inelegantly sprawled figure of the Professor, his ample body lying half propped against the base of the window seat.

"Professor!" Victoria shrieked, dropping to her knees beside the man, who now seemed to have slipped into unconsciousness. For one horrifying moment she thought she had rendered him into this woeful condition with the poker, until a quick inspection showed her that it had come to rest on the tip of his left foot, which must have been sticking out from under the hem of the draperies all along, if only she could have located it amid the mess.

Running her hands inexpertly over the Professor's body, she didn't take long to discover that there appeared to be a shallow, bloody depression imprinted in the back of his skull. As she probed the wound gingerly with her fingertips, Victoria's stomach did a curious flip when she felt a small piece of bone move slightly beneath her fingers.

"The skull is broken," she said aloud, then swallowed down hard, commanding her protesting stomach to take a firm hold on her breakfast and keep it where it belonged.

"Ooohhh!" the Professor groaned mournfully, moving his head slightly and then opening one eye, which seemed to take an unconscionably long time in focusing on the woman kneeling in front of him. Reaching out one hand, he grabbed her wrist painfully hard before whispering, "Find him! Find him! Make him pay!"

"Professor! Are you all right?" Even as she asked the question, Victoria acknowledged its foolishness. Of course he wasn't all right. He was most probably dying, and all she could do was ask ridiculous questions. She may have long since ceased feeling any daughterly love for the man now lying in front of her, but she could still be outraged that anyone would try to kill him. "Who did this to you, Professor?" she asked, feeling him slipping away from her.

"Find him, I said," the Professor repeated, his words slurring badly. "He has to pay...always...must pay...promise me...can't let him..."

"He'll pay, Professor, I promise he'll pay. I won't let him get away with it," Victoria declared dutifully, wincing as the hand enclosing her wrist tightened like a vise, as if the Professor had put all his failing strength into this one last demand for obedience. "But you must tell me who he is. Professor? *Professor!*"

The hand relaxed its grip and slid to the floor. Professor Quennel Quinton was dead.

CHAPTER ONE

As HE WAITED for the reading of the will to begin, the only sounds Patrick Sherbourne could hear in the small, dimly lit chamber were intermittent snifflings—emanating from a woman he took to be housekeeper to the deceased—and the labored creakings of his uncomfortable straight-backed wooden chair, the latter bringing to mind some of his least cherished schoolboy memories. He lifted his nose a fraction, as if testing the air for the scent of chalk and undercooked mutton, then looked disinterestedly about the room.

That must be the daughter, he thought, raising his quizzing glass for a closer inspection of the unprepossessing young woman who sat ramrod straight on the edge of a similar wooden chair situated at the extreme far side of the room, placing either him or her in isolation, depending upon how one chose to look at the thing.

No matter for wonder that Quennel kept her hidden all these years, he concluded after a moment, dropping his glass so that it hung halfway down his immaculate waistcoat, suspended from a thin black riband. The poor drab has to be five and twenty if she's a day, and about as colorful as a moulting crow perched on a fence.

She looks nervous, he decided, taking in the distressing way the young woman's pale, thin hands kept twisting agitatedly in her lap. Odd. Nervous she might be, but the drab doesn't look in the least bit grieved. Perhaps she's worried that her dearest papa didn't provide for her in his will.

That brought him back to the subject at hand, the reading of Quennel Quinton's will. *Professor* Quinton, he amended mentally, recalling that the pompous, over-weening man had always taken great pains to have himself addressed by that title, although what concern it could be to the fellow now that he was six feet underground, Patrick failed to comprehend.

The other thing that Sherbourne was unable to understand was the Quinton solicitor's demand for his presence in this tall, narrow house in Ablemarle Street, after one of the most woefully uninspiring funerals it had ever been his misfortune to view.

He had not met with Professor Quinton above three times in the man's lifetime—all of those meetings being at the Professor's instigation—and none of those occasions could have been called congenial. Indeed, if his memory served him true, the last interview had concluded on a somewhat heated note, with the irate Professor accusing Sherbourne of plagiarism once he found out that the Earl had entertained plans for compiling a history of his own and saw no need to contribute information to Quinton's effort.

Easing his upper body back slightly in the chair, he slipped one meticulously manicured hand inside a small pocket in his waistcoat and extracted his heavy gold watch, opening it just in time for it to chime out the hour of three in a clear, melodic song that drew him an instant look of censure from the moulting crow.

He returned her gaze along with a congenial smile, lifting his broad shoulders slightly while spreading his palms—as if to say he hadn't meant to interrupt the strained silence—but she merely lowered her curiously unnerving brown eyes before averting her head once more.

"Bloodless old maid," he muttered satisfyingly under his breath without real heat. "I should buy her a little canary in a gilt cage if I didn't believe she'd throttle it the first time it dared break into song."

"Prattling to yourself, my Lord Wickford? Bad sign, that. Mind if I sit my timid self down beside you? I feel this sudden, undeniable desire to have someone trustworthy about in order to guard my back. But perhaps I overreact. It may merely be something I ate that has put me so sadly out of coil."

Patrick, who also happened to be the Eleventh Earl of Wickford, looked up languidly to see the debonair Pierre Standish lowering his slim, elegant frame into the chair the man had moved to place just beside his own. "I didn't see you at the funeral, Pierre. It wasn't particularly jolly," Patrick whispered, leaning a bit closer to his companion. "By your presence, may I deduce that you are also mentioned in the late Professor's will?"

Standish carefully adjusted his lace shirt cuffs as he cast his gaze about the room with an air of bored indifference. "Funerals depress me, dearest," he answered at last in his deep, silk-smooth voice, causing every head in the room to turn immediately in his direction. "I would have sent my man, Duvall, here in my stead this afternoon, could I have but carried it off, but the Professor's solicitor expressly desired my presence. It crossed my mind—only fleetingly, you understand—to disappoint the gentleman anyway, but I restrained the impulse. Tiresome, you'll agree, but there it is."

He paused a moment, a pained expression crossing his handsome, tanned face before he spoke again in the same clear voice. "Tsk, tsk, Patrick. Can that poor, plain creature possibly be the so estimable daughter? Good gracious, how deflating! Whatever Quinton bequeathed to me I shall immediately deed over to the unfortunate lady. I should not sleep nights, else.''

Sherbourne prudently lifted a hand to cover his smiling mouth before attempting a reply. ''Although I am fully aware that you are cognizant of it, dare I remind you that voices rather tend to carry in quiet rooms? Behave yourself, Pierre, I beg you. The creature may have feelings.''

''Impossible, my darling man, utterly impossible,'' Standish replied quickly, although he did oblige his friend by lowering his voice ever so slightly. ''If it has feelings, it wouldn't be so heartless as to subject us to its so distressing sight, would it? Ah,'' he said more loudly as a middle-aged man of nondescript features entered the room and took up his position behind the Professor's scarred and battered desk. ''It would appear that the reading is about to commence. Shall we feign a polite interest in the proceedings, Patrick, or do you wish to abet my malicious self in creating a scene? I am not adverse, you know.''

''I'd rather not, Pierre—and you already have,'' Sherbourne answered, shaking his head in tolerant amusement. ''But I will admit to a recognition of the sort of uneasiness you are experiencing. At any moment I expect the proctor to come round, crudely demanding an inspection of our hands and nails as he searched for signs of poor hygiene. It is my conclusion that there lives in us both some radical, inbred objection to authority that compels us to automatically struggle against ever being relegated to the role of powerless standers-by.''

''How lovely that was, my dearest Patrick!'' Pierre

exclaimed, reverently touching Sherbourne's arm. "Perhaps even profound."

The solicitor had begun to speak, to drone on insincerely for long, uncomfortable moments as to the sterling qualities of the deceased before clearing his throat and beginning the actual reading of the will, the first part of which dealt with nothing more than a series of high-flown, tongue-twisting legal phrases that could not possibly hold Sherbourne's interest.

"I wasn't aware you were acquainted with old Quinton," Patrick observed quietly to Standish, having realized at last that Pierre had never sufficiently answered his earlier query on the subject. As if they were exchanging confidences, he went on, "Indeed, friend, I am feeling particularly stupid in that I have failed to comprehend why either one of us should be found unhappily present here today. For myself, I can only say that the good Professor did not exactly clasp me close to his fatherly bosom whilst he was above ground."

"I knew the man but slightly, untold years ago in my grasstime," Standish replied, adding smoothly, "though I had foolishly not thought to inform you of that fact. I trust, dearest, that you will accept my apologies for this lapse."

"Why not just call me out, Pierre, and have done with it?" Sherbourne asked facetiously, slowly shaking his blond head, as he should have known he couldn't get past Standish so easily. "And please accept *my* apologies for my unthinking interrogation. I was striving only for a bit of mindless, time-passing conversation. I assure you it was never my intention to launch an inquisition."

"Are you quite set against starting one, then?" Standish asked glumly, appearing quite crestfallen. "A pity. I begin to believe I should have welcomed the diversion—if not the thumbscrews. Our prosy friend behind the desk is not exactly a scintillating orator, is he?''

Just then Patrick thought he caught a hint of something the solicitor was saying. ''O-ho, friend, prepare yourself. Here we go. He's reading the gifts to the servants. We should be next, before the family bequests. What say you, Pierre? Do you suppose it would be crushingly bad *ton* if we were to spring ourselves from this mausoleum the moment we collect our booty?''

''*Shhh*, Patrick, I want to hear this. Oh, my dear man, did you hear that?''

''I'm afraid I missed it, Pierre,'' Patrick said, amused by the patently false concern on Standish's face.

''Quinton left his housekeeper of twenty-five years a miserly thirty pounds and a miniature of himself in a wooden frame!'' Standish pronounced the words in accents of outraged astonishment. ''One can only hope the old dear robbed the bloody boor blind during his lifetime.''

The solicitor reddened painfully upon hearing this outburst from the rear of the room, then cleared his throat yet again before continuing with the next bequest, an even smaller portion for the kitchen maid.

''As the Irish say, my dear Patrick, Quinton was a generous man,'' Pierre ventured devilishly. ''So generous that, if he had only an egg, he'd gladly give you the shell.''

This last remark was just too much—especially considering that the housekeeper, upon hearing it, gave out a great shout of laughter, totally disrupting the proceedings, while drawing Standish a chilling look from Miss Quinton. The angry solicitor removed his gaze from the document before him, prepared to impale the author of such blasphemy with a withering glare, but realized his

error in time. A man did not point out the niceties of
proper behavior to Pierre Standish—not if that man
wished to die peacefully in his bed.

Flushing hotly to the top of his bald head, the solicitor
quickly returned his attention to the will, reading importantly: "To Patrick Sherbourne, Eleventh Earl of
Wickford, I hereby bestow all my considerable volumes
of accumulated knowledge, as well as the research papers of a lifetime, with the sincere hope that he will, as
it befits his moral responsibility as an honorable gentleman, continue my important work."

"He never did!" came the incredulous outburst from
the housekeeper as she whirled about in her seat to look
compassionately at Professor Quinton's only child. "Oh,
Miss Victoria, I be that sorry!"

"Not half as sorry as I am," Patrick told Standish in
an undertone. "I shall have to build another library at
Wickford just to hold the stuff."

"If I might continue?" the solicitor asked as the
housekeeper's exclamation had set the two other occupants of the room—a miserably out-of-place kitchen
maid who was ten pounds richer than she had been that
morning, and a man already mentioned in the will and
identified as the Professor's tobacconist (and the recipient of all the Professor's extensive collection of pipes)—
to fidgeting nervously in their chairs.

"It's all right, Willie, honestly," Victoria Quinton
soothed softly, patting the housekeeper's bony hand.
"I'm sure the Professor had his reasons."

Wilhelmina Flint sniffed hotly, then said waspishly,
"He had reasons for everythin' he did—none of them
holdin' a thimbleful of thought for anyone save hisself."

"Enough! What's done is done. Please continue, sir."

Victoria said in a voice that fairly commanded the solicitor to get on with it.

"To Mr. Pierre Standish—who knows why—I bequeath in toto the private correspondence in my possession of one M. Anton Follet, to be found in a sealed wooden box presently in the possession of my trusted solicitor."

Upon hearing this last statement, Patrick stole a quick look at his friend, but could read no reaction on Pierre's carefully blank face.

"The remainder of my estate passes in its entirety to one Miss Victoria Louise Quinton, spinster. That's the last bequest," the solicitor told them, already removing his spectacles in preparation of quitting the premises. "Mr. Standish, I have the box in question, and the key, here on the desk. If you'd care to step up, I'll relinquish them as soon as you sign a receipt to that effect."

"My, my. Secret correspondence, Pierre?" Sherbourne suggested, looking at the other man intently. "Do you know this Follet fellow?"

"I know a great many people, Patrick," Standish answered evenly, already rising from his uncomfortable seat to bow slightly as the ladies quit the room, Miss Quinton in the lead, the uneven hem of her black gown sweeping the floor as she went. "Your recurrent curiosity, however, begs me ponder whether or not I should be performing a kindness by furnishing you with a comprehensive listing of my acquaintance, as a precaution against your spleen undergoing an injury, for example."

"Put m'foot in it again, didn't I, Pierre? And after I promised, too," Patrick remarked, grimacing comically at his faux pas. "I've no doubt you'll soon find me nattering with the dowagers at Almack's—lingering at the side of the room so as to catch up on all the latest *on-*

dits. I implore you—can you think how to save me from that pitiful fate? Perhaps, in your kindness, even suggest a remedy?''

''A diverting interlude spent in the company of young Mademoiselle La Renoir might prove restorative,'' Standish offered softly, accurately identifying Wickford's latest dasher in keeping. ''I hear the dear lady is inventive in the extreme—surely just the sort of diversion capable of ridding your mind of all its idle wonderings.''

''While ridding my pocket of yet another layer of gold, for La Renoir goes through her ingenious paces best when inspired by the sparkle of diamonds.'' The Earl shook his head in the negative. ''How jaded I have become, my friend, for I must admit that even Marie's seemingly endless repertoire of bedroom acrobatics have lost their ability to amuse me. I'd replace her, if not for the *ennui* of searching out a successor. My idle questions to you today are the most interest I have shown in anything for months. Perhaps I am past saving.''

''Er, Mr. Standish,'' the solicitor prompted, pointedly holding his open watch in the palm of one hand.

Standish ignored the man as if he hadn't spoken. ''Boredom can be the very death,'' he told Patrick sympathetically, idly stroking the thin, white, crescent-shaped scar that seemed to caress rather than mar the uppermost tip of his left cheekbone. ''I was bored once, my dearest, so you may believe that I know whereof I speak. Ended by wounding my man in an ill-advised duel, as a matter of fact, and nearly had to fly the country. That woke me up to the seriousness of my problem, I must say! Once free of the benighted bolt hole I had been forced to run for until the stupid man recovered— for a more cowhanded man with a sword you have yet to see—I vowed to show a burning interest in all that had been so nearly lost to me.''

''Such as?'' Patrick prompted.

''Such as, my darling Patrick, an extreme curiosity about the human condition, in all its frailties. Oh yes— I also acquired an even more intense concern for my own preservation.''

''I'd really rather not carve up some poor innocent, just to start my blood to pulsing with the thrill of life, if you don't mind, Pierre,'' Wickford pointed out wryly. ''Although I am sure that is not what you are suggesting.''

''What I am suggesting, darling, is that you look about yourself for some enterprise or pursuit that can serve to hold your interest for more than a sennight. In my case, the observation of my fellow creatures has proven to be endlessly engrossing. For you, well, perhaps Professor Quinton's papers will inspire you to complete his work.''

''Or prod me into slitting my throat,'' the Earl muttered, shaking his head. ''I do see your point, Pierre. I thank you, and I promise to give your suggestions my deepest consideration.''

Extracting a perfumed handkerchief from inside his sleeve, Pierre waved it languidly before touching it lightly to the corners of his mouth, saying, ''It was nothing, my darling man. But I'm afraid I really must leave you now, before our poor solicitor person suffers a spasm, dithering back and forth over the fear of offending me and his desire to return to his own hearth and slippers—although I fail to comprehend why anyone should fear me, as I am the most peaceful man in all England.''

''And I'm next in line for the throne,'' Sherbourne

responded playfully, to be rewarded by one of Standish's rare genuine smiles.

"*Et tu*, darling?" he commented without rancor. "Ah well, I imagine this common misconception of my character is just a cross I must bear. Pray keep me informed of your progress, my dearest Patrick, for I shall fret endlessly until I know you are restored to your usual good frame."

CHAPTER TWO

PATRICK REMAINED in his chair, idly watching Standish sign the receipt with a flourish and then depart, a small oblong wooden box tucked neatly under his arm. Perhaps he was desperate for diversion, but Patrick would have given a tidy sum to know the contents of that box. Pierre was a good friend, but not very forthcoming, and it was slowly dawning on Patrick just how little of a personal nature he really knew about Pierre Standish, even after serving with him in the Peninsula.

He looked around the book-lined room, wondering if M. Anton Follet was mentioned in any of the volumes, or in any of the papers holding Professor Quinton's extensive, although incomplete, history of the British upper class. His own research was devoid of any such reference, he knew, but then he had not gone much beyond a compilation of his and a half dozen other loosely related family histories before the whole idea had begun to pall and he had shelved the project (as he had so many others that he had begun in the years since his return to London from the war).

Rising stiffly from his chair—for he had spent the previous evening with Marie La Renoir and his muscles were still sending up protests—he realized that he and Miss Quinton, who had at some time reentered the library unnoticed by him to stand in the shallow window embrasure, were now the only occupants of the depressing room.

Steeling himself to pass a few moments in polite apology for having somehow usurped her claim on her father's life work (it would never occur to him that either he or Standish should apologize for their rudeness during the reading of the will for, in their minds, the crushing boredom of such an occasion had made them sinned against rather than sinning), he walked over to stand in front of her, a suitably solemn expression looking most out of place on his handsome, aristocratic face.

"Miss Quinton," he began carefully, "I can only tell you that your father's bequest came as a complete surprise to me. As I could not but help overhearing your housekeeper's refreshingly honest reaction at the time, I can only assume that you had a deep personal interest in his work."

Victoria Quinton turned around slowly to look at the Earl levelly, assessingly—dismissively. "Yes, you would have assumed that, wouldn't you?"

Patrick blinked once, looking at the young woman closely, unwilling to believe he had just been roundly insulted. She was standing stock-still in front of him, her hands clasped tightly together at her waist, the picture of dowdy dullness. He had to have been mistaken—the woman hadn't the wit to insult him. "I assure you," he then pressed on doggedly, "if there are any papers you particularly cherish—or any favorite books you would regret having pass out of your possession—you have only to mention them to me and I will not touch them."

"How condescending of you. In point of fact, sir, I want them all," Victoria Quinton replied shortly. "Indefinitely. Once I have discovered what I need to know, Lord Wickford, you are welcome to everything, down to the last bit of foolscap. Make a bonfire of it if you wish.''

Not exactly the shy, retiring sort, considering her mousy exterior, Sherbourne thought, his curiosity reluctantly piqued. Possessing little that would appeal to the opposite sex, she had probably developed an animosity toward all men; no unmarried miss of his acquaintance would dream of speaking so to him. ''Would it be crassly impolite of me to ask what it is you hope to discover?'' he asked, staring at her intently.

Victoria turned smartly, her heavy black skirts rustling about her ankles, and headed for the hallway, clearly intending to usher her unwelcome visitor to the door. ''It would be, although I am sure you feel that being an earl makes you exempt from any hint of rudeness. But I shall nevertheless satisfy your curiosity, considering your generosity in allowing me use of the Professor's collection. I shall even pretend that I did not overhear your complaints when you first heard of the bequest.''

Patrick's dark eyes narrowed as he stared after this infuriating drab who dared to insult him. ''How kind of you, Miss Quintin,'' he drawled softly as they stopped walking and faced each other. ''I vow, madam, you fair bid to unman me.''

Miss Quinton's left eyebrow rose a fraction. ''Indeed,'' she pronounced flatly. ''As I was about to say, sir: I have dedicated myself to the unmasking of the man who murdered the Professor. The answer lies in his papers, and I shall not rest until the perpetrator is exposed. And now, good day to you, sir.''

She then moved to stand beside the open door that led down three shallow steps to the flagway lining the north side of Ablemarle Street. But her startling disclosure (and jarring candor) had halted Wickford—who could only view departing the house as his single most cherished goal in life—in his tracks, leaving him standing some distance from the exit.

"Find the murderer?" he repeated, not trying very hard to hide his smile. "How very enterprising of you, madam. Have you perhaps looked underneath your bed? I hear that many spinsters believe murderers lurk in such places."

Victoria's chin lifted at the insult. "I'm positive you are considered quite amusing by your friends in those ridiculous clubs on St. James's Street, but I can assure you that I am deadly serious."

"But your father was killed by a burglar he must have discovered breaking into his library," Patrick pressed on, caught up in the argument against his will. "Murder, yes, I agree, but it's not as if the man's identity could be found amid your father's research papers or personal library. I fear you will have to resign yourself to the sad fact that crimes like this often go unpunished. Law enforcement in London is sorry enough, but investigations of chance victims of violence like your father are virtually nonexistent."

The front door closed with a decided crash as Victoria prepared to explain her reasons to the Earl—why, she did not stop to ask herself—so incensed was she by his condescending attitude. "The Professor knew his murderer, probably opened the door to him, as a matter of fact. I have irrefutable evidence that proves my theory, but no one will listen to me. I have no recourse but to conduct my own investigation."

"What is your evidence?" Patrick asked, feeling a grudging respect for her dedication, if not her powers of deduction.

"That, Lord Wickford, is of no concern to you," she

told him, pulling herself up to her full height. As she spoke she slipped a hand into the pocket of her gown, closing her fingers around the cold metal object that was her only lead toward discovering the identity of the murderer. "Suffice it to say that I have in my possession a very incriminating clue that—while it does not allow me to point a finger at any one person—very definitely lends credence to the theory that *you,* sir, or one of a small group of other persons I shall be investigating with an eye toward motive, entered the Professor's library as a friend and then struck him down, leaving him to lie mortally injured. Before dying in my arms the Professor charged me with the duty of bringing his murderer to justice and, I say to you now in all sincerity, sir, that I shall do just that! All I ask of you is some time before you remove the collection. I will notify you when I no longer require it."

"Admirable sentiments, eloquently expressed, Miss Quinton," Patrick owned soberly, "although I feel I must at this point protest—just slightly, you understand—that you have numbered me among your suspects."

Bats in her belfry, Patrick then decided silently, becoming weary of the conversation. That's what happens to these dusty spinster types after a while. But aloud, he continued, "I'll respect your right to hold to your own counsel about your 'clue,' of course. But my dear Miss Quinton, you must know that I would be shirking my duty as a gentleman if I didn't offer you my services should you find yourself in need of them. That is, if you are willing to accept help from one of your suspects?"

"I shan't need your help," Victoria retorted confidently, deliberately ignoring the vague feeling of unease that had been growing ever since she first began this strange conversation. Longing to do Sherbourne an injury, she thought to herself: If I cannot throw actual brickbats at him, I can at least attack him verbally. "For now," she continued in a voice devoid of emotion, "it is enough that I have been able to interview my first suspect. I might add, sir, that I shall strive not to allow your boorish behavior today—and all I have read in the newspapers about your questionable pursuits—to prejudice me against you. At the moment, you are no more suspect than any of the other gentlemen who could have committed the crime.

"I apologize for baiting you so openly, Lord Wickford," she then conceded, her voice softening a bit, "but you are only the second suspect I have encountered today, you understand, the first having escaped before I could speak with him. I was merely testing your responses, feeling you out as it were," she added, not entirely truthfully, for in fact her opinion of him and his kind was not especially high.

Now Victoria had Sherbourne's complete attention. "Second suspect, you say? As I doubt that either the solicitor or that down-at-the-heels tradesman who scurried out of here with the Professor's collection of pipes is capable of murder, could you possibly be trying to tell me that Pierre Standish is also to be considered a suspect? My, my," he remarked, seeing the answer on her expressive face. "At least, Miss Quinton, you have put me in good company, although I imagine I should be feeling quite put out with you for even supposing I could have had anything to do with your father's death, except for the fact that I find it extremely difficult to take seriously anything you have said. Your last revealing statement implicating Mr. Standish has served to confirm my opinion of the worthlessness of your arguments."

Patrick smiled then, shaking his head in disbelief. "Therefore, I won't even dignify your assumption of my possible guilt with a question as to your reasons for it. I make no secret of my disagreement with your father when last we met, as I realize it is more than possible that you overheard us."

"I have not yet been able to ascertain a motive for you, or any of the suspects," Victoria was stung into saying. "To tell the truth, there may still be suspects I have not yet discovered. I am in no way prepared at this time to make any accusations."

"I shall sleep better knowing that, at least for now, you are only *assuming* to place guilt rather than running off to the authorities with a demand for my immediate arrest, I assure you," Patrick returned, bowing with an insulting lack of respect. "I shall also—need I even say it?—make it a point to enlighten Mr. Standish of his new status as a suspect in a murder, although telling him that he is not unique in his position, but has merely been lumped in with other would-be dastards, may not be a wise move on my part. Pierre does so hate running with the herd, you understand. But I'm sure you won't let Mr. Standish's righteous anger frighten you if he should happen to take umbrage at your accusation, for your motives are pure, aren't they, Miss Quinton? After all, you are only doing as any loving daughter might do, and you *are* a loving daughter, aren't you, Miss Quinton?"

Victoria's pale face became even more chalklike before a hot flush of color banded her features from neck to forehead—the only portions of her anatomy Patrick could, or wished to, see—and she replied coldly, "My feelings for and relationship with my late father are not at issue here, sir. The Professor was murdered, and I have undertaken the fulfillment of a dying man's last wish. It's the only honorable thing to do under the circumstances.''

Patrick looked about the drab hallway consideringly. ''You've led a rather quiet, almost sequestered life, Miss Quinton. Dare I suggest that you are contemplating using the Professor's death as an excuse to insert a bit of excitement into your previously humdrum existence? Although, looking at you, I can't imagine that you possess any real spunk, or you would have asserted yourself long since rather than live out your life in such dull drudgery, catering to the whims of an eccentric, totally unlikable man like the Professor. No, I must be mistaken. Obviously you believe yourself to be embarked on a divine mission. Do you, perhaps, read Cervantes?''

''This is not some quixotic quest, sir, and I am not tilting at windmills. I have control of my mental faculties, and I am determined to succeed. I suggest we terminate this conversation now, so that I may get on with my investigation and you may repair to one of your ridiculous private clubs, where you can employ that inane grin you're wearing to good use as you regale your low-life friends with what I am sure will be your highly amusing interpretation of my plans and motives.''

Sherbourne's smile widened as he shook his head in disbelief. ''I really must read the columns more often, if their gossip has indeed painted me as black as you believe me to be. At the very least, such a vice-ridden, pleasure-mad libertine as I should be enjoying himself much more than I think I am, don't you agree? Either that or—oh, please say it isn't so—you, Miss Quinton, have hidden away behind that dreary gown and atrocious coiffure a rather wildly romantic, highly inventive, and suggestible mind that is considerably more worldly than your prim façade, educated speech, and high-flown ideals indicate.

Is that why you're so hostile, dear lady? Are you a bit *envious* of those lives you read about in the scandal sheets? Are you out to snare a murderer to fulfill the Professor's dying wish, or do you see this as a chance to deliver a slap in the face to a society that you equally covet and despise?''

"That's not true!" Victoria exclaimed, aghast. "How dare you insinuate that I have ulterior motives for my actions? You don't know me. You know less than nothing about me." The Earl's verbal darts were striking with amazing accuracy now, and all Victoria could think of was finding some way to make him leave before she could be tricked into saying something that confirmed his suspicions. "Every word you utter convinces me more that you are the guilty party—attacking blindly in the hope you will somehow be able to dissuade me from my intentions. Let me tell you, sir, yours is an exercise in futility! I shall not be defeated by such an unwarranted personal attack!"

"As you say," Patrick answered, one finely arched eyebrow aloft. "Well, good hunting, Miss Quinton. If you desire any assistance, or need rescuing when you find yourself in over your head, please do not hesitate to contact me."

"I find it incumbent upon me to say that I cannot think of what possible use *you'd* suppose yourself to be," Victoria marveled nastily, "considering your reputation for the aimless pursuit of pleasure, not to mention your renowned propensity for immature exploit."

"Oh no, you misunderstand, Miss Quinton," the Earl informed her mildly. "I shan't come pelting into the fray on my white charger to *save* you, you understand, but I might be inclined to wander by and say 'I told you so' on my way to some nearby low gaming hell or depraved orgy." Moving once more toward the door, he added, "Now that we have exchanged the requisite pleasantries, I do believe I shall take my leave. Do please try not to weep as I pass out of your life forever, Miss Quinton. I'd wager a considerable sum that yours is not a face that would be enhanced by a maidenly show of tears."

"I never cry" was all Victoria answered, bent on correcting his misconception without seeming to take exception to his ungentlemanly remarks. The only outward sign that his insult had hit a tender spot was to be found in a slight widening of her curiously amber eyes, but it was enough to afford Patrick some small solace.

"I can believe that, Miss Quinton," he answered cheerfully, patting his hat down on his head at a jaunty angle as he prepared to leave before she said something that tried his overworked patience too high. "I imagine any emotion save your obvious contempt for your fellow man to be alien to one such as you. Indeed, it must gratify you in the extreme to be so superior to the rest of us poor mortals. When your father's papers pass into my possession—in other words, on the day when you finally are forced to admit defeat in your 'quixotic quest'—I shall be eager to inspect the Quinton family tree. It must be thick with truly outstanding specimens."

"You have not heard me boast of my ancestry, sir. It is you who carry a coat of arms on your coach door like a badge of honor, as if anything any of your ancestors has done can possibly reflect advantageously on you, who have done nothing to deserve the slightest honor at all."

Patrick's back stiffened as he swallowed down hard on an impulse to strangle the unnatural chit. He hadn't yet gotten through her iron-hard shell, no matter what he had thought earlier. He hadn't found a single chink in her armor of dislike and indifference that had refused to yield even an inch. She should be reduced to tears, not standing there toe-to-toe with him, trading insults.

"When first I saw you, Miss Quinton, I thought your father hid you away because of your lack of looks," he offered now, knowing he was behaving badly but somehow unable to help himself, for the woman seemed to bring out the worst in him. "I see now I was sadly mistaken. It was your serpent's tongue he strove so hard to conceal. Hasn't anyone ever told you it's not nice to go around antagonizing people with every other word that rolls off your agile tongue?"

Victoria took in the heightened color in Lord Wickford's thin cheeks and decided that she had tried him high enough for the moment. He had revealed nothing of himself save a reluctance to admit to anger and an ability to trade verbal insults without flinching, and he had appeared truly surprised to hear of her belief that her father had known his murderer.

Even so, she should have considered her tactics more closely before deciding to opt for a full, frontal assault. After all, hadn't Willie always told her that one caught more flies with honey than with vinegar? Victoria winced inwardly, wondering if the Earl was right—that she was, at three and twenty, taking on all the less-than-sterling traits of the waspish spinster.

Of course, she comforted herself, his surprise could have just as easily stemmed from his realization that she had somehow discovered some evidence that could incriminate him, she amended carefully, knowing it wouldn't be prudent to jump to any conclusions this early in the day.

She was just about to open her mouth and apologize for having behaved so shabbily when Sherbourne, who had just interrupted his latest move toward the front door as a sudden thought occurred to him, whirled to point a finger in her face and demand: "Pierre Standish, Miss Quinton. Humor me, if you please, and speculate for just a moment—what possible reason could *he* have had for putting a period to your father's existence?"

"Who is M. Anton Follet, Lord Wickford?" was Victoria's maddening reply.

Patrick inclined his head slightly, as if acknowledging a flush hit. "Ah, madam, such deep intrigue. I do so love cryptic questions, don't you?" His smile was all admiration as he ended silkily, "If this is a sample of your sleuthing, however, I suggest you repair to your knitting box without further delay."

"I don't knit."

Patrick's eyes closed in a weary show of despair. "This, I believe, is where I came in. *And,* madam, this is where I depart. Good day to you, Miss Quinton."

So saying, Sherbourne opened the front door and let it close softly behind his departing back.

It wasn't until his coach (the one with the gilt coat of arms on the doors) had delivered him to his own doorstep that Sherbourne realized he was more than just extremely angry. He was also confused, upset, and intensely curious about Pierre Standish, M. Anton Follet, Quennel Quinton, Miss Victoria Quinton's bizarre scheme, and the identity of the Professor's murderer.

It did not occur to him that the one thing he was not was bored.

CHAPTER THREE

"WHAT AN ODIOUS, odious man!" Victoria Quinton told the empty foyer once the Earl of Wickford had departed, having gained for himself—although it pained her, she had to acknowledge it—the last, telling thrust in their war of words. For at least one fleeting moment during their conversation she had felt the same impotent fury she had invariably experienced on the rare occasions when she had gone up against the Professor in a verbal battle before she had at last decided that she really didn't care enough about her father's view of life to try to convince him of her side on any subject.

Crossing the foyer to enter the small, shabby drawing room that—as the Professor had rarely visited it—she considered her own, Victoria walked over to stand directly in front of the wall mirror that hung above a small Sheraton side table, one of the few fine pieces of furniture that her mother had brought to the marriage.

The mirror hanging above it, on the other hand, was a later purchase of the Professor's, and it was exquisite only by way of its ornate ugliness. Peering through the virtual forest of carved wooden decoration that hemmed the mirror in from all sides, Victoria did her best to examine the features she saw reflected back at her.

"'Not a face that would be enhanced by a maidenly show of tears,'" she quoted, tilting her head this way and that as she leaned closer for a better view, as Victoria was markedly shortsighted without the spectacles she had chosen not to wear that afternoon.

"What Lord Wickford left unsaid was that if I had been so foolish as to ask him what would enhance my looks, he would have immediately suggested the prudent disposition of a large, concealing sack overtop my head." She smiled in spite of herself, causing a dimple Patrick Sherbourne had not been privileged to see to appear in one cheek, lending a bit of humanizing animation to her usually solemn face.

Putting a hand to her chin, she turned her head slowly from side to side once more, objectively noting both her positive and negative features. "The eyes aren't all that depressing, if I can only remember not to squint at anything beyond the range of ten feet." she mused aloud. "Although I do wish my brows were more winglike and less straight. I always look as if someone has his hand on the top of my head, pushing down."

Squinting a bit as she moved almost nose to nose with her reflection, she continued her inventory. "Nose," she began, wrinkling up that particular feature experimentally a time or two. "Well," she concluded after a moment, "I do have one, not that it does much more than sit there, keeping my ridiculously long eyes from meeting in the middle, while my skin certainly is pale enough to pass inspection, although I do believe I should have considerably more color than this. In this old black gown I look less like one of the mourners and more like the corpse."

She stepped back a pace and deliberately pasted a bright smile on her face, exposing a full set of white, even teeth surrounded by a rather wide, full-lipped mouth that did not turn either up or down at the corners. Her neck—a rather long, swanlike bit of construction—

did not seem to be sufficiently strong to hold up her head, and her small, nearly fleshless jaw, though strongly square boned, perched atop it at almost a perfect right angle, with no hint of a double chin.

Reaching a hand behind her, she pulled out the three pins holding up her long, dark brown hair, so that it fell straight as a poker from her center part to halfway down her back. "Ugh," she complained to the mirror, ruefully acknowledging that, although her hair was a good length, it was rather thin, and of a definitely unprepossessing color. "How could anyone with so much hair look so bald?" she asked herself, trying in vain to push at it so that it wouldn't just lay there, clinging to her head like a sticking plaster.

Then, holding her hands out in front of her, she inspected her long, slim, ink-stained fingers and blunt-cut nails before quickly hiding them again in the folds of her skirt. The Professor had told her repeatedly that her hands and feet were a disgrace, betraying physical frailty because of their slender, aristocratic construction.

"How I longed all through my childhood for a knock to come at the door and for someone to rush in to tell me that I wasn't really Victoria Quinton but a princess who had been stolen away by gypsies and sold to the Professor for a handful of silver coins," she reminisced, smiling a bit at the memory. Having no real recollection of the mother who had died while her only child was still quite young, Victoria had resorted to fantasy to explain away her unease at being unable to love the strange man who was her father. "Oh well," she acknowledged now with a wide grimace, "if my aristocratically slender bones didn't gain me a royal palace, at least they saved me from being hired out as a dray horse in order to bring a few more pennies into the house."

That brought her to the point she had been dreading, an inventory of her figure. "What there is of it," she said aloud, giving an involuntary gurgle of laughter. Victoria might have inherited her above-average height from the Professor, but she had been blessed—or blighted, according to the Professor, who would have liked it if she could have been physically suited for more of the housekeeping duties—with her mother's small-boned frame and inclination to thinness.

"Skinny as a rake, and considerably less shapely," she amended, as her reflection told her clearly that the only things holding up her gown were her shoulders.

Victoria closed her eyes for a moment, sighed deeply, then lifted her chin and began twisting up her hair, fastening the anchoring pins with a total disregard for the pain her quick movements caused. "Point: Victoria Quinton, spinster, is an antidote," she declared, staring herself straight in the eyes. "Point: Mr. Pierre Standish insulted me openly and then all but cut me dead. Point: The Earl of Wickford did not hesitate in revealing to me his distaste for women of my sort." She stopped to take a breath, then ended, "Point: I don't care a snap about the first three points.

"Mr. Standish is a soulless devil, everyone knows that, and the Earl—well, he is the most excessively disagreeable, odious man I have ever met, not that I have even spoken to above two or three of that unimpressive gender in my entire life. I don't care a button what they think, and I am well shed of the pair of them!" She nodded her head decisively and her reflection nodded back to her.

She felt fairly good about herself and her deductions for a moment or two, until her mind, momentarily blunted by this rare display of self-interest, stabbed at her consciousness, rudely reminding her that she *did* need them. If she were ever to solve the puzzle of just who murdered the Professor, she needed them both very much.

Even worse, she acknowledged with a grimace, she needed to do something—something drastic—about making herself over into a young woman who could go about in public without either spooking the carriage horses or sending toddlers into shrieking fits of hysterics.

The two men who had been in the house in Ablemarle Street were not her only suspects—although they did for the moment stand at the head of the list of society gentlemen she had thus far compiled—and she must somehow inveigle introductions to certain others of the *ton* if her plan to ferret out the murderer was to have even the slimmest chance of succeeding.

Victoria pressed her fingertips to her temples, for she could feel a headache coming on, and looked about the room, searching for her spectacles. She still felt slightly uneasy about her decision not to wear the plain, rimless monstrosities, unwilling to recognize maidenly vanity even to herself, and decided to blame the insufferable Earl of Wickford, and not her foolishness, for the dull thump-thumping now going on just behind her eyes.

How she longed for her cozy bed and a few moments' rest, for she had been sleeping badly ever since the Professor's death three days earlier, but she discarded the idea immediately. "The Professor would have kittens if I dared to lie down in the middle of the afternoon," she scolded herself sternly. Although she had never been afraid of the man, she had found it easier to keep her thoughts to herself and display an outward show of obedience, thus saving herself many a lecture.

But then, just as she was about to head for her work-basket that stood in the corner and the mending that awaited her there, she brought herself up short, and a small smile lit her features. ''And who's going to run tattling to him, Miss Quinton, if you do take to your bed—Saint Peter? You are your own mistress now, my dear,'' she reminded herself, a bit of a lilt coloring her voice. ''You have longed for this day, dreamed about it for years, and now—through no fault of your own—it is here. You are free, Victoria Quinton, free to do whatever you will!''

Pivoting smartly on the heels of her sensible black kid half boots, she exited the small drawing room in a near skip, heading for the staircase.

It was perhaps only a small act of rebellion after so many years of doing only what she was told, but it was to set a precedent for the future.

CHAPTER FOUR

PATRICK HALTED on the threshold of the club's sedately decorated main salon and looked about for Pierre Standish, finally locating his quarry sitting alone and looking very much at his ease near one of the large floor-to-ceiling windows that overlooked the busy street below.

Sherbourne did not take himself immediately to that side of the room. Instead he spent several minutes wandering about in a seemingly aimless fashion, passing the time of day with some of his friends, although declining to sit and take refreshment with any of them.

He even took the time to place a wager with Lord Alvanley on the outcome of a mill that was to be held in the countryside later that week, before eventually arriving at his planned destination and sliding into a facing wing chair, a jaunty greeting on his smiling lips.

"Tsk, tsk. That took you precisely three minutes longer than it should have, my darling Patrick, although, in general, it was rather well done," Standish drawled amicably before returning his large gold watch to his pocket and looking up at Sherbourne for the first time.

"I beg your pardon, Pierre?" Patrick questioned, keeping a carefully blank look on his face as he adjusted his coattails before crossing his legs at the knee, allowing one elegantly fashioned Hessian to dangle.

"Yes, I believe you should," Standish answered smoothly as he motioned to a servant who was hovering nearby to fetch another glass for his lordship. "I recall that I have urged you to find an interest, my darling, but I fear your future does not lie in cloak-and-dagger machinations."

Patrick shook his head in admiration, admitting defeat. "How did you know I was looking for you particularly? I thought I was being quite smooth, actually."

Pierre took up the glass the servant had brought and poured some rich-looking red liquid into it from a decanter before handing the glass to Wickford. "I could, I suppose, say I have visited a wizened old gypsy in Europe who—because of some heroic service I rendered her—has given me the gift of foretelling events, causing you to look at me in awe, but honesty prevents me. Actually, dearest, I was at home when you called this morning but—how shall I say this without being indiscreet?— I was considerably engaged at the time."

Taking a small sip of his wine, Patrick leaned back in his chair and quipped mischievously, "My deepest apologies. I can only pray that I didn't interrupt at a critical moment? Some *indiscretions* have so little understanding of the link between concentration and performance."

Pierre's dark eyes twinkled slightly in his otherwise emotionless face. "I have amazing powers of concentration, thankfully. Besides, Patrick, you know I have always made it a point never to disappoint a lady."

Patrick acknowledged his understanding with a slight nod of his head, knowing better than to dwell on the subject. Besides, he had not sought out Standish merely to spend a few pleasant minutes enjoying the verbal sparring that helped pass the time between noon and an evening's entertainment. "Speaking of ladies, Pierre—"

"Not I, my dear, at least not literally," Standish said, a smile still lurking in his eyes.

Patrick chose to ignore this last statement, knowing that Pierre could keep a conversation jogging along in this lighthearted vein forever, without once saying anything to the point. He had met with his friend for a reason, and it was time the two of them got down to serious business. "There's something I think you should know, Pierre. Miss Quinton believes her father knew his murderer," he announced baldly, watching his friend closely for any reaction.

Pierre did not so much as blink. "How utterly amazing. I am, of course, astonished," he said in a tone that totally belied his statement.

"As usual, my friend, you react by not reacting. Perhaps a bit more information is required." Leaning forward a bit so that he could speak without fear of being overheard, he went on confidingly, "Does the fact that this same Miss Victoria Quinton considers you and me to be her prime suspects pique your interest in the slightest?"

"Are we, by God?" Standish responded, raising his dark brows a fraction. "I begin to believe you have awakened a slight curiosity on my part—perhaps even the faint glimmerings of interest. Perhaps you will oblige me by beginning with how you have come upon this charming little tidbit of information."

Patrick leaned back in the chair once again, satisfied at last with his friend's response. "The lady in question told me herself the day of the funeral, not that she wanted to, you understand."

"It's that pretty face, Patrick," Pierre interrupted, an earnest expression on his dark face. "I've noticed before the devastating way you have with the ladies. I imagine you've heard quite a few things over the years. Have you ever thought of writing your memoirs?"

"It was not my pretty face that did it, but her own satisfaction with her deductions that had her flinging her outlandish theory at my feet like a gauntlet," Sherbourne corrected testily. "Lord, man, at first she attacked me like a hound on a blood scent, trying, I believe, to frighten me into confessing."

"Quite the little Trojan, hmmm?"

"Quite the little idiot," Patrick amended. "She's taken it into her head to solve the mystery of the Professor's murder, you see, and believes the answer might lie somewhere in the papers I've inherited."

"And your thoughts on the subject?" Standish prodded, reaching for his wineglass.

Patrick smiled slightly, shaking his head. "I think the lady in question is a bit queer in her attic. Quinton was killed by a burglar; everybody knows that."

"Do they?" The question held no inflection, hinted of no hidden curiosity. It was just as if Standish, like Miss Quinton, had thrown out a suggestion, and now was waiting to see if his friend was going to pick it up.

Patrick slowly twirled the glass in his hand by its slender stem, watching the small bit of wine swirl around the bottom in a tight whirlpool as he considered Pierre's question. At last he raised his head a fraction, staring intently into the other man's eyes.

"Yes, darling?" Standish purred.

"Victoria Quinton may have the disposition of a cursed warthog—and a face to match—but she's sharp as needles, Pierre. Much as it pains me to admit it, I can't simply dismiss her assertions as daughterly grief. It's—it's as if she considers what she's doing as some sort of *duty*. Do you know, Pierre, I don't think she loved Quinton—or even *liked* him."

"Quennel Quinton was many things as I recall, but I

know *I* did not find him to be especially lovable. Perhaps I have underestimated our little drab. She must have some intelligence,'' Pierre put in thoughtfully.

Patrick nodded in agreement. ''A dedicated bluestocking, I'd say, which is why I cannot comfort myself by believing her theory to be some romantic bag of moonshine she's embraced merely in order to lend some sparkle to her humdrum existence. She's just not that sort of female.''

Pierre directed a long, dispassionate stare at the man facing him before speaking again, all trace of mockery now gone from his voice. ''You seem to have given our dowdy Miss Quinton and her assertions quite a bit of thought, Patrick. Perhaps you have even begun to question the reasons behind the Professor's demise yourself. Tell me, my dear, is this to be an intellectual exercise only, or do you plan to do something about it?''

Patrick lapsed into silence once more, absently raising his wineglass to take a drink before realizing it was empty, and then holding it out as Pierre refilled it from the decanter. Lifting the glass to his lips, he then downed its contents in one long gulp before rising to his feet. ''She's a damned obstinate woman, Pierre, and she's deadly serious about this foolishness she's taken into her head. Somebody has to watch out for her, or she'll land in a scrape for sure.''

Pierre put down his glass and applauded softly. ''Congratulations, my darling man. You have come to exactly the correct decision. But do be careful, Sir Galahad— lest the lady decides to view her benefactor in a romantic light. You may save her from carelessly falling into the hands of a desperate murderer, only to have her end up casting herself into the Thames for love of you.''

''Don't worry about that, Pierre,'' Patrick assured

him. "Victoria Quinton hates the sight of me. She thinks I'm a terrible, shameless person. Useless too, I believe she said."

"I wait with bated breath, my dear one, to hear your opinion of her opinion."

Patrick slipped a snow-white lace handkerchief from his cuff and daintily dabbed at the corners of his mouth in imitation of one of his friend's little affectations before answering: "I was flattered, of course, my dear Pierre. What else could I be?"

CHAPTER FIVE

"YOU'RE LOOKING kinda peakedlike, Miss Victoria," Wilhelmina Flint remarked a week after the Professor's funeral as she lifted yet another stack of papers from the desk in the library in order to run her feather duster over its shiny surface. "Why don't I run myself on down to the kitchens and brew you up some of my black currant tea onc't I'm all finished puttin' this mess to rights?"

"Finish it, Willie?" Victoria questioned lightly, leaning back in the Professor's big leather chair to look up at the hovering housekeeper. "The only way this room could possibly get any cleaner would be if you were to dump all the furniture into the garden and whitewash the walls. Didn't you just dust in here this morning?"

Willie raised her chin and sniffed dismissively, although she wasn't really offended by her young mistress's words, considering that she had raised Miss Victoria since the girl was just out of soggy drawers and had therefore long ago become accustomed to her genial attempts to belittle her own love of cleanliness and order.

"Go away with you now, Missy," she said, going on with her work, which for the moment meant she was concentrating on chasing down yet another daring bit of lint that had somehow escaped her eagle eyes earlier.

While Wilhelmina tidied and fussed and generally stirred up more dust than her switching feathers could capture, Victoria sat at her ease, idly observing the hubbub as she gratefully abandoned her increasingly disquieting research for a few moments. Willie was a treasure, even with her seeming obsession with cleanliness, and Victoria knew it, just as she knew that the woman must never learn so much as the slightest hint of damning information coming to light about her longtime employer.

Although the housekeeper—who had left the countryside to be with her mistress in London when the Professor took the local squire's only daughter to wife—had never tried to replace Victoria's dead mother in her heart, Wilhelmina's brisk efficiency had always been liberally laced with affection for the plain, awkward child who received nothing but the most cursory notice from her busy professor father. If Victoria confided in her now, Wilhelmina would put a halt to the murder investigation immediately!

Victoria had grown to love the tall, rawboned redhead, and as she grew older she had secretly coveted Willie's buxomy, wide-hipped, narrow-waisted, hourglass figure, believing the housekeeper's ample curves and brilliant coloring to represent the epitome of feminine beauty.

Even now, with the once vibrant red hair showing traces of grey, Victoria could still see much of the full-blown beauty that had once been Wilhelmina's, and wondered yet again why she had never married. Surely there must have been plenty of opportunities. ''Willie,'' she ventured now, ''tell me truly—there must have been someone you wished to wed, maybe some farmer back in Sussex before you moved here? I mean, you didn't stay with us all these years just because of me, did you?''

The housekeeper stopped in the midst of rubbing a brass bookend with a corner of her starched white apron and peered intently at the serious young woman. "Because of you, Miss Victoria?" she questioned in a tone that hinted at the utter ridiculousness of such a question, then laughed out loud. "Lord love you, Missy, I should most certainly think not! It's crazy in love I was with the dear, sweet Professor, of course. That's why I stayed. It's as plain as the nose on your face!"

Now it was Victoria's turn to laugh, for if there were ever two people born to do murder to each other they were Wilhelmina Flint and Professor Quennel Quinton. Clearly Willie was doing her best not to load her young mistress down with yet another heavy dose of guilt, to be piled atop all the other guilt she was feeling over being unable to muster up any genuine grief over her father's death.

"I may have led a sheltered life, Willie, but I'm not a complete greenhead," Victoria reminded the housekeeper, sobering again. "You and the Professor were many things to each other, but none of them were even remotely connected to anything of a romantic nature."

"You're forgettin', Missy. The Professor left me that fine miniature of hisself. Wouldn't you be wonderin' why he should do such a thing?"

Victoria sat front once more, placing her elbows on the desk. "That's another thing that puzzles me, Willie. There's something about that miniature that bothers me. I don't ever remember seeing it before, for one thing, but it's my inability to reconcile the miniature with the man I knew that is most difficult. I imagine it is hard to conjure up a real sense of recognition when faced with an image of one's parent at an age closer to one's own."

Willie backed hurriedly away from the desk, turning her body slightly away from Victoria's as she extracted a cloth from one of her apron pockets, and then pro-

ceeded to make a great business out of dusting one of
the uncomfortable wooden chairs that comprised the
only seating for visitors in the room. "Doesn't quite look
like the old geezer, does it? It'd be the smile that's
throwin' you off, I wager, Missy, seein' as how he did
precious little of it in his lifetime."

Victoria allowed a small, appreciative grin to show on
her face before prudently hiding it with her hand. Willie
had always been fairly outspoken about her lack of love
for the Professor during his lifetime, but now that the
man was gone she seemed to be pulling out all the stops.
If she only knew... But no, Victoria didn't dare tell her.

"I won't scold you, Willie, even though I must remind you that you are being disrespectful of the dead.
You have every right to be upset over the pittance he
left you after all your years of service," Victoria went
on, urging further confidences. "Even Mr. Pierre Standish—although he was extremely rude to voice his opinion aloud—said that thirty pounds was a most sorry
sum."

"It was thirty pounds more than I was expectin',
Missy," Wilhelmina replied, flicking her cloth briskly
over the seat of the chair before sitting herself down with
a thump and looking her mistress straight in the eyes.
Victoria suppressed the sudden urge to flee, knowing
that somehow the tables had been turned and Wilhelmina was about to ask some very probing questions of
her own.

"What I wants to know now, Miss Victoria, is this—
how much did the cheeseparin' old skinflint set by for
you? I've been watchin' you and wonderin' what it is
that's put you so badly off your feed. You've been sittin'
in here day in, day out for over a week now, shufflin'

those papers back and forth from one pile to another. It's bad news, isn't it?''

Victoria hesitated a moment, wondering if it was exactly fair to pour out at least a part of her troubles to Willie, who could do nothing more than commiserate with her—other than to throw a few colorful curses the Professor's way, of course—but she did feel a great need to talk to somebody.

"Well," she began slowly, a note of bitter self-mockery in her tone, "as you must know, Willie, there existed between the Professor and myself a certain, er, want of openness while he was alive."

"He treated you like an unpaid servant, lovin' and trustin' none but hisself and his useless scribblins'," Wilhelmina cut in candidly. "Let's call a spade a spade, Missy. There's naught but ourselves here to listen, you know."

Victoria lifted her head, throwing her long, slim neck and clearly defined, fragile, square jaw into prominence. "You're right, Willie, as usual," she said with some asperity. Then, losing a bit of her bravado, she began to ramble, hoping to change the subject. "It's time to call a spade a spade, whatever that silly saying means, for whatever else would one call it—a flowerpot? Willie, did you ever stop to consider just how silly some of our time-honored sayings are? Like 'right as a trivet.' Whatever could that mean? Could it just as easily be 'left as a trivet'? Or 'wrong as a trivet'? After all—"

"Are we soon goin' to be servin' tea in the parlor to the sheriff's officers?" Willie interrupted brusquely, not about to be sidetracked now that she had nearly gotten her mistress to the sticking point.

"You mean like Lord Barrymore did years ago, Willie?" Victoria asked, obviously still more than eager to digress from the distasteful subject of her current financial embarrassment. "I read somewhere in the Professor's notes that Lord Barrymore was dunned so much that the sheriff's officers seemed as much at home in his house as did his own servants."

Wilhelmina nodded impatiently. "Yes, yes. His lordship had them dress up as servants when he was throwin' a party. I know all about it, Missy. Us that serve know everythin'. Now stop tryin' to twist out of it and tell me—are we rolled up?"

It was no use, Victoria decided, opening her mouth to speak. "The Professor held the purse strings entirely, of course," she began slowly, "and I doubt even you could find anything unusual about that."

"Not out of the way, Missy, just stupid," Wilhelmina answered baldly. "As if there was yet a man born who knew the real cost of things—yellin' for fresh peas in the dead of winter like I was goin' to take m'self off out into the back garden and find 'em hangin' on the trees."

"But although he kept the household on quite a strict budget," Victoria pressed on, wishing to get over this rough ground as smoothly as she could, "*he* always seemed to have funds enough to purchase his expensive books and his favorite tobaccos and, of course, his finely aged brandy. Oh dear, that sounded rather condemning, didn't it?"

"He knew how to live, that he did. I'll say that much for him," Wilhelmina put in thoughtfully. "I can't say I liked his choice of tailors, with the dull as ditchwater browns that he fancied for everything, but the quality was always there, wasn't it?"

Victoria nodded her head up and down firmly, as if Willie's confirmation of her assessment of the Professor's finances had reinforced her own feelings. "Naturally I assumed that the Professor had some private form of income—monies invested in the Exchange, or some income from an inheritance. You know what I mean.''

Wilhelmina sat forward at attention. ''But?''

''But his solicitor tells me he has no record of any such matters, and I have searched and searched this room without unearthing a single clue as to where the money came from. Even this house is rented.''

Wilhelmina's expressive brows came together as she frowned, considering what she had just heard. ''Are you tryin' to tell me that the old bas—, um, that the Professor left you without a penny to scratch with? I can't believe it! It doesn't make a whit of sense, Missy.''

''Oh, there's some money in the house,'' Victoria explained hastily. ''I found nearly one hundred and fifty pounds locked in a small tin box in the bottom drawer of his desk. There's more than enough to honor the Professor's bequests to you and Betty, and the rent for this quarter's already been paid. If nothing else, at least I didn't find any unpaid tradesmen's bills.''

''So there's naught but a hundred pounds standin' betwixt you and the street?'' Wilhelmina pursued intently, shaking her head in mingled anger and disgust. ''You keep my thirty pounds. I've got more than enough put away that I don't need to be takin' the bread out of a child's mouth. Lucky thing for old Quennel that he's dead, let me tell you, for I'd like to strangle him with my own bare hands, and then go off to the hangman singin'!''

Victoria looked around the library at all the books the Professor had purchased over the years. ''If only he hadn't chosen to leave the collection elsewhere,'' she said, sighing. ''I'm sure I could have realized a considerable sum on its sale.''

''The Earl didn't seem like he was over the moon to have been landed with the dusty stuff,'' Wilhelmina pointed out helpfully. ''I'd be willin' to wager he could be talked into givin' it all back to you if you was to ask him.''

Victoria fairly leaped from her chair to cross the room and look out the window at the small garden, hiding her flushed cheeks from the housekeeper's all-seeing eyes. ''That man is utterly abominable!'' she shot back with some heat. ''I wouldn't ask the Earl of Wickford for a stale crust of bread if I were starving in a gutter!''

''Which you might very well be, Missy, if you don't rid your foolish head of this notion you've taken into it about finding the Professor's murderer,'' Wilhelmina supplied archly. ''Better you spend the next few months sniffin' around for a husband to take care of you, I say.''

''A husband! I have not the least expectation of such a thing!'' Victoria, pulling a face, cried indignantly. ''Oh, maybe once or twice—long ago—I had the usual dreams about falling in love with some handsome gentleman and living happily every after. But I'm three and twenty, Willie, and well past the usual age for marriage, even if I were so coldhearted a person as to seek matrimony simply as a way to save myself from having to make my own way in the world like any honest woman. Besides,'' she added, spreading her arms as if to invite Wilhelmina's inspection of her unprepossessing appearance, ''who do you propose as a suitable match for someone like me—the rat catcher?''

The housekeeper jumped to her feet, a quick flush deepening the color in her naturally rosy cheeks. ''Now see here, Missy, there's nothin' the matter with you that a bit of good food and some fresh air wouldn't put to rights! You're the spittin' picture of your blessed mother—Lord rest her soul and forgive her for being so weak as to allow herself to be married off to Quennel Quinton like she did—and she was a truly beautiful lady.''

Victoria's dark amber eyes softened as she shook her head slowly in the negative. ''Ah, Willie, you're a wonderful friend to me, truly you are. But then you didn't get to hear Lord Wickford's blighting assessment of my charms—or should I say my lack of them.''

''Knowing you, Miss Victoria, you probably laid him out in lavender with that sharp tongue of yours before his lordship even had the time to look at you.'' At Victoria's involuntary wince, Wilhelmina pressed her point home. ''Men are not so knowin' as they think they are, you understand. First you must present them with a pretty package—only then will they take the time to tug on the ribbons, like, and look a little deeper. Once he got to know you as I do, Lord Wickford would be like warm butter in your hands.''

Victoria walked back over to the desk and sat down wearily. ''I don't know, Willie. That description sounds rather messy to me. Besides, I don't like Lord Wickford. He's as shallow and vain…and…and arrogant as the rest of his sort. I have no desire to gain his approbation. I'd as lief retire to the country and raise dogs, really I would. But first I want to—that is, I *must* keep my promise to the Professor.''

''That again!'' Wihelmina exploded. ''You owe that man nothin'—less than nothin' now that you know he left you without a feather to fly with. You have two months, or about that, before you must give up this house. Better to spend the time in thinkin' of yourself—not that selfish old man. Dyin' he was, and all he could think of was havin' you go harin' off to find out who did him in. You'd think that a body who knew he was about to meet his Maker would have a few thoughts about the poor innocent child he was about to leave behind. It's a bleedin' pity, that's what it is.''

Victoria pressed the knuckles of her closed fist to her mouth, fighting against the pain Wilhelmina's passionate words caused to clutch at her chest. The Professor had never once acted in an affectionate way toward his only offspring, so it would have been totally out of character for him to have had a kind word or two for her as he lay dying, but Victoria was human enough to have wished for more from her father.

In time Victoria, using the vivacious Wilhelmina as a yardstick against which to judge herself, had decided that she was the homely, helplessly ugly specimen the Professor said she was, and had therefore made no demur when he chose to have her dressed in nothing more colorful than mud brown and kept her closeted inside summer and winter, much to the detriment of her pale complexion.

If anything, Patrick Sherbourne's scathing description of her appearance—added to that of Pierre Standish—had put the final seal on her opinion of herself as being a truly undesirable female. She had a good brain—not even the Professor could quibble with that—but that brain told her that Wilhelmina's suggestion that she hang out her hopes for a husband was nothing more than an impossible dream.

No, Victoria told herself, reaching out blindly to pick up the first page of one of the stacks of paper lying in front of her, there existed unrealistic goals and attainable goals. Marriage was an unrealistic dream. Victoria was resigned to spending her life as one of the invisible people, destined to observe the world from the sidelines, in the role of governess, or perhaps as a spinster schoolteacher.

But before she resigned herself to the deadly dull existence that she felt to be her destiny, Victoria would take one slight detour into the world of excitement and intrigue, just as Patrick Sherbourne had so accurately surmised. She would play Bow Street Runner and ferret out the man who had murdered the Professor. She owed it to him, she comforted herself, having given him her solemn promise she would do it. But that wasn't really why she was looking forward to her investigation.

Opening the middle drawer of the desk, she slipped a hand inside to draw out the small enameled snuffbox Wilhelmina had found on the floor of the library the morning the Professor was discovered lying there injured. Holding the thing up to the light, she turned it slowly this way and that, admiring the detailed workmanship that had gone into the finely etched initials carved into its lid.

"P.S.," she read aloud, her eyes narrowing into slits as she contemplated just what those initials could mean. "Patrick Sherbourne. Pierre Standish. Somehow I hope it was one of them rather than any of the others I have discovered so far, for I do believe I would thoroughly enjoy handing over evidence condemning either of those gentlemen."

Wilhelmina shook her head in mingled dismay and disgust. "It's a sorry day, it was, that I showed you that snuffbox. I would have turned it over to that bumblin' constable if I had but known you'd take it into your head to think the thing belonged to the murderer."

"It has to, Willie," Victoria reminded the housekeeper. "Just think about it a moment. You clean this house almost hourly, bless you, so that snuffbox never could have escaped your broom unless it was dropped that same night by the murderer. I'm sure the Professor knew his killer; he just died before he could tell me who it was. After all, whoever it was had all night to ransack the library and find the box with the Professor's money in it. No burglar would have left empty-handed—only a man who had no need of funds would have done so.

"There's absolutely no doubt in my mind," Victoria said confidently, placing the snuffbox back into the drawer. "This is a very important clue, and it will lead me to the murderer, of that I am convinced. My only problems presently are money and time. I fear I may not have enough of either to do what must be done."

Wilhelmina had been still long enough. Reaching down to retrieve her cleaning rag, she began dusting the bookshelves even as she continued her arguments as to the impossibility of Victoria ever succeeding in her plan. "You'd have to go about in Society to rub up against folks like Lord Wickford and Mr. Standish, Missy. That takes money—money you don't have. It also takes knowin' the right people. You don't know anybody but me, and—lordy—I haven't been invited to sit down to tea with the Queen in ages."

Victoria allowed herself to be amused by Wilhelmina's small joke, but the housekeeper's bald truths could not be laughed away. "You're right, Willie. It's a difficult task I have set myself. Isn't it a shame I have no fairy godmother to come wave her wand over me and turn me into a rich, beautiful princess? It certainly would make things considerably easier, wouldn't it?"

FIVE HOURS LATER, Victoria closed the old journal with a snap and pushed it away from her before propping her elbows on the desk and lowering her chin into her hands.

After her first, early successes in compiling a list of likely suspects she had somehow thought it would be only a matter of time before all the remaining pieces of the puzzle fell into place and she could identify the murderer.

But as the list of suspects grew, so too did the questions concerning exactly what the Professor had been up to, locked away in this library year after year. After all, aside from a few widely spaced magazine articles, his work had never been published—so what exactly was the source of his income? If he had no investments, no allowance from some inheritance she had never heard of, then she was at a loss to explain how they had lived in the relative comfort they had enjoyed all these years.

Victoria had also learned that the Professor had no arrangement with any publisher in the city concerning the publication of his "definitive history," which, as his transcriptionist, she knew to be years away from completion, so there was no point in pursuing that avenue in the hopes he had been receiving funds in anticipation of future profits.

"Still didn't find anything to the point, did you, Miss Victoria?" Wilhelmina observed as she reentered the library after finishing her own luncheon in the kitchen, shaking her head as if to say, I knew you wouldn't. "You should be out lookin' for a husband, and not sittin' in here diggin' into these dusty old books."

"Oh Willie, this is impossible!" Victoria complained, tucking a stray lock of hair behind her ear. "If I thought the Professor's manuscript was dull, let me tell you, his personal journals make them sound like racy novels in comparison."

"Like that Mrs. Radcliffe's *An Italian Romance,* what I found tucked in a hatbox, sittin' alongside your best bonnet?'' Wilhelmina asked as she flicked her feather duster over a row of books sitting on the corner of the Professor's desk. ''Mayhap I shoulda snuck in here of an evenin' and read some of his stuff m'self.''

Retrieving the journal and placing it on the top of a small stack of similar books before slipping them all into a large side drawer, Victoria replied regretfully, ''Alas, it was only a figure of speech, Willie. The Professor's writings, both public and private, were all as dry as dust. His journals ramble on for page after page about the most everyday things—as if the price of tallow candles in 1799 should be preserved for posterity.''

''At least you won't have to go worryin' yourself that his lordship, the Earl of Wickford, will be readin' all about the Professor's wild and wicked past,'' the house-keeper offered, abandoning her dusting in order to run a finger along one of the windowsills, just to check up on the housemaid's efficiency.

''Wicked past? Willie, you know as well as I that the Professor's life was as ordinary as plain pudding. Why else do you think I have been reduced to reading Mrs Radcliffe?'' Then, remembering just what Wilhelmina had said about discovering her latest hiding place for her lending library books, she went on: ''About that hatbox, Willie—''

''I was just tidyin' things up a bit, Missy,'' the house-keeper put in hastily. ''You know how lazy that Betty is. Why, if I'm not on her all the time, I swear she'd do nothin' more than wave kisses at the dirt as she breezed by. Did I tell you how I found her last week? There she was, plain as day, washin' down the front steps with—''

''That hatbox was at the very back of my wardrobe, secreted behind a dozen other boxes,'' Victoria per-sisted, knowing that Willie's love of cleanliness and order, and not nosiness, lay at the heart of the matter, but not adverse to seeing the housekeeper squirm a bit in her attempt to explain her motives. "There are times, Willie, that your dogged pursuit of demon dirt fairly boggles the mind."

Wilhelmina lifted her chin and assumed an injured air. "Well, you don't have to hit me over the head to make me know that you're pokin' fun at me, Miss Victoria. And me that's raised you since before you could so much as walk upright. Your darlin' mother gave me this position, and I have to say myself that I've served very well, but if you are wishful of makin' changes in the staff now that the old man got his notice to quit, why, I guess I can go to m'sister in Surrey."

Victoria stood up and came around the desk to slip an arm around the older woman's shoulders. "You'd leave me, Willie?" she asked mournfully, resting her head against the side of Wilhelmina's ample bosom. "You know I was only teasing, don't you?"

"Here now," Wilhelmina scolded, disengaging her mistress's arm before she succumbed to the urge to cradle Victoria in a motherly embrace as she had done years ago. "That'll be enough of that, Missy. Besides," she continued after she had snatched up her feather duster and launched an attack on another row of books, "now that the Professor isn't here to naysay anything, you can keep your books anywhere you want to, right?"

Victoria leaned back against the front of the desk, a slowly widening smile lighting her features as she contemplated the bookshelves as they would look when lined with row after row of her books—volumes that would reflect her deep love of art, music, and fine literature. "I'll keep Mrs. Radcliffe on a top shelf, though, Willie, just so as not to injure some visitor's sensibilities," she decided, beginning to enjoy the thought of at last being her own mistress. But the smile faded as she remembered that hers was to be a short-lived independence.

"At least we won't be pinching pennies quite yet, Willie. I found another hundred pounds, stuck between the pages of one of the Professor's daily journals I was reading this afternoon," she told Wilhelmina now, for the time had more than passed to keep secrets from the housekeeper.

"Did you now?" Wilhelmina observed, peering around the room as she contemplated the fortune that could be concealed between the covers of Quennel Quinton's extensive collection. "Do you suppose the money belongs to Lord Wickford now?"

Crossing her arms militantly across her chest, Victoria responded loftily, "The will said he was to get the collection. It mentioned nothing about anything hidden in the collection. Besides, he'd do nothing more lofty with the funds than to spend them on some painted dancer from Covent Garden or some such thing. No! I shall use the money to investigate the murder. I'm sure that's what the Professor would have wished me to do."

"Quennel Quinton never wished for anyone to do anything with money," declared a deep voice, "except give it to him so he could squirrel it away—and you know it, Willie Flint!"

"By the holy Peter!" Wilhelmina Flint screeched, throwing up her hands in dismay.

Victoria turned fearfully toward the doorway at the familiar tone of the man's voice, only to see the Professor standing just at the edge of the rug.

"Good afternoon, ladies. The door was open, so I let myself in," he said, just before Victoria Quinton, who had always thought herself above such missish displays, slid gracefully to the floor in a swoon.

CHAPTER SIX

VICTORIA RETURNED to consciousness slowly, her first thought concerning the fact that she was somehow lying down on the drawing room settee in the middle of the day with her shoes on. Her second thought was—naturally—that Willie would tear a wide strip off her if she could see her acting with such callous disregard toward the furniture.

Then vague memories of what had transpired in those last moments before her swoon sent her blood to pounding through her veins, and she opened her eyes a fraction, calling tentatively, "Professor?"

"Not likely" came the amused answer, and she turned her head warily on the pillow to peer at the elegantly clad man standing in the middle of the room.

"You!" she bit out, swinging her legs to the floor so that she could come to a sitting position, a move that sent the room spinning slightly before her eyes for a moment. "*Ohhh,* my poor head! What are you doing here, sirrah? How dare you remain alone in a room with an unconscious female? Have you no decency at all?"

Patrick Sherbourne, unruffled by this outburst, walked leisurely toward a small armless chair near the settee and sat down before deigning to answer. "You are correct, Miss Quinton, to point out my lapse in observing the proprieties."

"I should certainly hope so!" she said primly, arranging her skirts over her knees.

"However," he went on, undaunted, "in my own defense I must say that I have in the past had occasion to be alone in other rooms with other horizontal females, so you may see why I did not realize my error sooner." He paused a moment—for effect, Victoria was certain—then added, "Of course, none of them were *unconscious* at the time, you understand. After all, I do have my reputation to maintain, don't I?"

Victoria's hands clenched into fists as she fought to take hold of her temper before it got the better of her, causing her to disgrace herself by picking up the statuette on the table in front of her and ramming it firmly into Lord Wickford's left ear. "I withdraw my observation on the proprieties, sir. Clearly I am wasting my breath pointing out any impropriety to one such as you. But I would like to ask you a question, if I may?"

"You may," Patrick agreed, "although I cannot promise to have the answer at my disposal. I've just arrived, you see. The front door opened at my knock—it was slightly ajar—and after debating a bit I decided it would be best if I entered and ascertained for myself whether or not there was anything amiss. After all, the burglar may have come back for a second go-round, mightn't he?"

"And I was just lying in here—alone?" Self-consciously, Victoria raised a hand to assure herself that her black mourning gown was still securely buttoned up to her throat. "Weren't you worried that I had been murdered?"

Patrick carefully removed a small speck of lint from his pantaloons and held it up to the light. "That distressing thought had occurred to me, but of course I dismissed it at once," he answered languidly. "You see, drawing on what I'd gleaned from our initial meeting, I deduced that there isn't a single soul in all the British Isles with enough moral courage to try to harm so much as a single hair on your head."

"Indeed," Victoria said tartly.

"Yes, indeed. It would take a braver man than I to attempt to overpower you, Miss Quinton. Why, your tongue alone could slice a man to ribbons before he could muster a counterattack. Then there's your appearance…"

Victoria sat up very straight and glared at him from between narrowed eyelids. "And what, pray tell me, is so very intimidating about my appearance?"

Patrick ran his gaze over her figure, from her untidy topknot to the heavy black shoes sticking out from beneath the hem of her woefully out-of-fashion gown, and shuddered delicately. "Please don't force me, Miss Quinton. After all, I *am* a gentleman."

"Miss Victoria! You're awake!" Wilhelmina burst into the room like a whirlwind, a small glass vial held high in one hand and a damp cloth clutched in the other. "I was that worried when you fainted, not that I blame you, for I don't. I made Quentin wait in the library after he carried you in here, so you wouldn't wake just to see his ugly puss and go off again. Here, dearie, take a sniff of this," she ended, dropping to her knees beside the settee and taking the stopper out of the vial.

"Oh, take it away, Willie!" Victoria begged, pushing the bottle back from her nose as the stinging fumes brought tears to her eyes. But Wilhelmina's mention of someone named Quentin brought her up short, and she grabbed the housekeeper's other wrist to hold her there.

"I thought I saw the Professor come into the library, didn't I, Willie?"

Victoria's grip was painfully tight on Wilhelmina's wrist, and the housekeeper hastily bobbed her head up and down in the affirmative, hoping her answer would result in her freedom before her hand turned blue. "Yes, yes, Miss Victoria, you thought you saw the Professor," she agreed, tugging hard until at last her wrist was free. "Lord, you've got quite a grip for such a scrawny thing, child."

"Strong men quail before her, that's what I've heard," Sherbourne put in silkily as he helped the housekeeper to her feet, and Victoria grumbled something unintelligible under her breath.

"Here, now," said a voice from the door. "Take your hands off my beloved, or prepare to defend yourself!"

"Beloved!" Wilhelmina scoffed, tossing her head so that her heavy mane of greying red hair shifted slightly in its pins. "That's a round tale, Quentin, if ever I heard one."

Both Patrick and Victoria were struck speechless by the sight of the man who was now standing in front of Wilhelmina, an ingratiating smile lighting his face.

At first sight there was no reason for either of them to believe they were seeing anyone but Quennel Quinton, but a few moments of careful observation banished that disquieting thought from both their heads.

Quennel Quinton had been a rather tall, portly man of about five and fifty years, with blue eyes and a blond fringe of hair ringing his otherwise bald head. The man Wilhelmina had addressed as Quentin was his exact double physically, except perhaps for the fact that his blue eyes seemed to sparkle with mischief, his rounded cheeks were as rosy as two ripe apples, and his mouth was arranged in an unabashed grin—something Quennel Quinton's mouth had never seemed able or willing to produce.

And there any attempt at making a comparison between the two men came to an abrupt end. Where Quennel had been sober, almost funereal in his dress, Quentin was clad in loud, flamboyantly styled emerald-green satin, with half a dozen gold chains spanning his considerable stomach. Three glittering rings pinched the pudgy fingers of both of his hands and a diamond as large as a pigeon egg nested in his cravat.

No, this certainly couldn't be Professor Quennel Quinton come back from the grave—not unless being tucked up temporarily underground had served to addle his senses beyond measure.

Quentin stood very still, seeming to enjoy the fuss his presence was making, as Patrick, quizzing glass stuck to his eye, walked in a slow circle around the man, inspecting him like a tout assessing a possible Derby entry, while Victoria, still sitting perched on the edge of the settee, openly goggled at him, her mouth slack.

"You're a relative, of course," Patrick said at last, allowing his quizzing glass to drop. "I don't believe we saw you at the funeral."

"Yes," Wilhelmina cut in, obviously not in the mood to kill the fatted calf for this supposed returned prodigal. "So seein' as how you're too late to either steal the pennies off his eyes or the brass nails from his coffin, why did you bother to come, Quentin? There's no money for you, you know. Not a single bent brass farthin'."

Quentin turned to Patrick, a sad smile on his face. "Ain't exactly tumblin' over herself to welcome me back, is she?" he asked blithely. "Ah well, it's not like

I was expectin' her to fall on my neck weepin' with joy, you know. Give her time, your lordship, that's what I say. I know she still loves me.''

"Love you? Love you!" Wilhelmina shot back heatedly. "You left me to rot while you went off chasin' rainbows. Snuffed my love like a candle, that's what you did. So if you think you can just come trippin' in here after all this time and call me your love, *Mr.* Quinton, let me tell you—''

Quentin winked at Sherbourne. "See? I told you. She's crazy in love with me.''

"Oh, fie on you, Quentin Quinton!" Wilhelmina cried, flapping her great white apron a time or two in a shooing motion before raising it to cover her flaming cheeks as she ran from the room like a hysterical young girl.

All this time Victoria had been sitting there, her eyes going back and forth from Quentin to Wilhelmina to Patrick, like a helpless spectator trying her best to keep watch on a flying shuttlecock during a game of battledore, unable to summon up so much as a single question that had anything to do with the conversation then taking place. But now, with the housekeeper gone (taking with her the disquieting thought that the woman had a torrid romance hidden in her past), Victoria at last found her voice.

"Who—who are you?" she asked hollowly.

Sherbourne patted her on the shoulder in a maddeningly brotherly way. "Not a very original question, my dear Miss Quinton, and certainly not up to your usual standards, but I do believe you are heading in the right direction."

Turning her head slowly so that she could look directly into Wickford's eyes, she pronounced two words slowly and distinctly: "Go...*away*."

"Here, now, young'un, is that any way to talk to his lordship?" Quentin scolded, looking from one to the other of the young people in consternation, finally directing his bright blue eyes at Sherbourne. "You are a lordship, ain't you, young fella? You look like a lordship."

"Patrick Sherbourne, Earl of Wickford, at your service," Patrick admitted, bowing in Quinton's direction. "My compliments, sir, and those of my tailor, who has repeatedly told me that clothes do make the man."

Quentin smiled again, clearly delighted to be in the presence of an earl, and held out his beefy, beringed hand. "Quentin Quinton, if you don't already know it. It's a pleasure to meet you, my lord."

Victoria stood up, exasperated beyond belief at the polite exchange taking place between the hated Wickford and this strange man who must surely be related to her, heaven only knew how. "Isn't this all just too pleasant for words," she bit out sarcastically. "Shall I ring for the tea tray now, or do you wish for me to withdraw so that the two of you can have a pleasant coze in my drawing room?"

"Feisty little thing, ain't she?" Quentin asked Patrick before lowering his considerable bulk into a nearby chair, whose springs protested loudly under the strain. "Reminds me of her mother, bless her dear departed soul, although she doesn't seem to have poor Elizabeth's looks. Pity. I had hoped—"

The sound of a heavy object hitting the far wall with some force brought Quentin up short, and both he and Patrick turned to look at Victoria, who was still on her feet, and looking more than a little incensed. "Will you please tell me who you are? I feel as if I've been somehow transported to Bedlam. Look what you made me do!''

Shebourne obligingly looked in the direction she was pointing and saw the heavy book that now lay against the base of the wall, its spine badly splintered. ''Elizabeth, then, was also a bit overvolatile?'' he asked Quentin placidly, ignoring the fact that Victoria was standing not two feet away from him, her hands clenched into tight fists.

''Not exactly overvolatile, your lordship,'' Quentin corrected, ''but game as a pebble, dear Elizabeth was. Never did understand how she ended up with Quennel, but her father arranged the marriage, and there was nothing the poor child could do to gainsay it.''

''Ohhh!''

''You screeched?'' Sherbourne asked Victoria, who had just dropped heavily back down onto the settee, her amber eyes flashing fire. ''Really, Miss Quinton. I know you are not in the custom of receiving visitors, but even the most elementary show of good manners seems to be beyond you. You are to entertain guests, not quiz them or—most definitely—subject them to the sight of ugly temper tantrums. Perhaps you should withdraw, just until you can gain control of yourself.''

Quentin chuckled his appreciation of Sherbourne's wit, but his face sobered as he looked at the girl, who appeared to be on the verge of hysterics—or murder. ''Victoria, my dear child,'' he said, frowning, ''please forgive me for shocking you and then ignoring you. But I must say, I was a bit surprised that you refused to call me Uncle. I know your father and I didn't exactly get on over the years, but—''

''Uncle?'' Victoria interrupted, slowly shaking her

head. "I believe I must have misunderstood you, sir. The Professor had no brothers."

Quentin's troubled expression cleared as at last he understood Victoria's confusion and the reason he had not been informed of his brother's death. "No brothers, is it, niece? Well, tell me now, how do you like this? The departed Quennel was not only my brother, but my *twin* brother. I'm the older by five minutes," he added, turning to Sherbourne.

"And may I say you also were the recipient of all the looks and personality," Patrick replied, clearly amused. "I don't mean to pry, Mr. Quinton, but perhaps you will be good enough to answer one question. Where have you been keeping yourself, if Miss Quinton here has never heard of your existence?"

Quentin reached up to scratch at the bit of blond fuzz that sat above his left ear. "Well now, your lordship, that's a long story, and I'm feeling a mite parched. Victoria, do you think you could scratch up something in the way of some liquid refreshment for your poor black-sheep uncle?"

Victoria was still feeling disoriented, still struggling to take in what she had just heard. "I—I imagine I could have Willie make some tea," she offered weakly, never thinking to offer any of the Professor's private stock of brandy as she herself had never known the taste of strong spirits.

"Tea! That'd be the day. I should have known Quennel wouldn't have any good wine in the house. Cheap as a clipped farthing, that was my dear brother," Quentin retorted, winking at Patrick as he reached a hand inside his jacket and pulled out a flat silver flask. "Just fetch us a couple of glasses, niece. Right, your lordship?"

Patrick couldn't remember the last time he had been so diverted. Whether it was the flask or Victoria's ridiculously shocked expression at the sight of it that set him off, even he couldn't have said, but suddenly he found himself lying back against the chair cushions, laughing out loud.

CHAPTER SEVEN

"AND THAT'S ABOUT IT, your lordship. Quentin married Elizabeth and the two of them traveled straight here to London, with my darling Willie coming along after leaving a message for me warning me never to darken her door again unless I was willing to give up my reckless ways."

Victoria and Patrick had been listening with great interest for nearly an hour as Quentin told them about his checkered youth in Sussex. The only sons of an impoverished, widowed cleric, Quennel and Quentin Quinton had been raised in a drafty, run-down rectory, dependent on Elizabeth's father, the local squire, for their daily bread.

Quennel had been a model son, if a bit dour for someone of his tender years, while Quentin had seemed to be the spawn of the devil, forever landing in scrapes from which his beleaguered father would have to extricate him. The only constant about Quentin was his devotion to Wilhelmina Flint, daughter of the local innkeeper, who was the most beautiful girl in the village, save Elizabeth, the squire's daughter.

"We were close as inkle-weavers once, Willie and me, if you take my meanin', your lordship." Quentin had told Patrick, giving the Earl a broad wink that caused a bit of pink to steal into Victoria's pale cheeks. "But I was a frisky colt, always on the go and wanting to see a bit of the world before I was ready to work in harness. So when Quennel and Elizabeth married, Willie went with them to London, leaving while I was gone from the village doing—well, it doesn't matter what I was doing, does it? After all, my niece is present, isn't she?''

Quentin was not very forthcoming on the courtship of Quennel and Elizabeth, merely saying, ''There's no accounting for tastes, is there?'' even if he himself did think it was ''a rum business all around.'' But the squire had a disky heart and probably wanted his only child settled before he was taken off, and heaven only knew Quennel wanted her. ''Quennel always took a shine to what he knew he shouldn't have,'' Quentin had told Victoria, who had not responded, but only sat on the settee in shocked silence.

''Well,'' Quentin had gone on jovially, as he had taken recourse to his flask more than a few times during his little talk and was feeling quite relaxed and at his ease, ''when I came home from one of my jaunts, m'father met me at the door with the news of Quennel's marriage and Willie's departure and wouldn't even so much as let me across his threshold. Told me I'd end in the workhouse, or worse, what with my feckless, adventuring ways, and sent me about my business without so much as a civil goodbye. Let me tell you, I went away a crushed man—forsaken by all I loved—and it took me more than a half dozen years before I even tried hunting down Willie and m'brother here in the city.''

''And by that time Elizabeth was dead and Willie refused to leave the young Victoria?'' Patrick had ventured, gaining himself a vigorous nod from Quentin, who was just then wiping a tear from his eye with a large white handkerchief.

Feeling a bit overset, Quentin had ended his story only a few moments later, and the trio had sat in silence for some minutes, each thinking his own thoughts.

Suddenly Victoria came out of the near trance she had been in since Quentin had begun speaking. "Of course! That miniature the Professor left Willie in his will. It wasn't of him—it was of you!"

"Sent it to her from India along with a proposal of marriage and enough blunt for a one-way fare to join me," Quentin confirmed, looking confused. "Shipped it all off right after I made my first fortune. Why did Quennel have it?"

Patrick got to his feet and walked slowly across the room to look out the window that faced Ablemarle Street. "You know," he said reflectively to no one in particular, "I do believe it begins to look like Professor Quennel Quinton was not a particularly nice man. Mr. Quinton," he went on slowly, turning to face the other man, "I think it might be safe to suppose that your beloved Mrs. Flint never received your proposal—or the money for her fare to India."

"No! That's utterly preposterous, even for the Professor! I will not have you, a veritable stranger, speak so about him," Victoria objected quickly, hopping to her feet to glare accusingly at the Earl. "How dare you! You're an abominable, arrogant, and thoroughly odious man to suggest such a thing."

"On the contrary, Miss Quinton," Patrick corrected silkily, smiling at her in such a maddeningly sympathetic way that she longed to box his ears. "Being abominable, arrogant, and—what was that last brick you tossed at me?—oh yes, and odious, I am in the perfect position to recognize one of my own. Your father, you poor lamb, seems to have been a rotter of the first water. Keeping a man away from his true love, tsk, tsk. I do believe I might weep.''

''You have no proof—''

Quentin raised a hand to place it soothingly on Victoria's forearm, gently pushing her back onto the settee. ''Tell me, my dear,'' he asked quietly, ''did you enjoy the books I sent you from Rome? And the lace and perfume I had shipped from France? Perhaps the ivory-sticked fan from Spain was your favorite? No? There were more gifts over the years, many more, but I can see from the look on your face that you never saw them. Wickford,'' he called softly, ''do you think you could hunt up another glass? I do believe my niece here could use a swallow or two from my flask.''

CHAPTER EIGHT

VICTORIA DIDN'T KNOW if she was on her head or on her heels. One moment she had been a penniless orphan, soon to be cast into the street with nowhere to go, no one to turn to, and the next she had been somehow transformed into the fortunate niece of one Quentin Quinton (late of the East India Company), a truly extraordinary man who wore pigeon-egg-sized diamonds in his cravat and prattled about presenting Victoria to Society as a well-dowered (if slightly long in the tooth) debutante.

Now, lying in her bed at the end of a most trying day, she thought back to the conversation that had taken place in the drawing room just before the Earl of Wickford had at last taken his leave of the premises.

"I believe the two of you should be alone to discuss these family matters," he had said once he had procured a glass for Victoria, filled it to the brim, and placed it into her trembling hand. "Although it has been heartwarming in the extreme to witness this joyous meeting, I begin to feel somewhat *de trop*. Quinton, it was a pleasure to meet you—a true pleasure—and I can only hope that you will bid me welcome if I chance to find myself in Ablemarle Street in the future."

Sherbourne, Victoria remembered now with a grimace, had then bowed to the both of them and taken his leave, lingering only long enough to toss a verbal bomb into the room by saying, "I suggest you have your intrepid niece tell you about her plans to collar the Professor's murderer, dear sir. It makes, I vow, for very interesting listening.''

Victoria sat up in bed and reached behind herself for her pillow, which she punched a time or two with her fist before laying both it and herself down once more. ''Oh, what a thoroughly insufferable man!'' she said feelingly. ''It wasn't enough for him to have been privy to the fact that the Professor kept me ignorant of my uncle's very existence. It wasn't sufficient revenge for him to have the satisfaction of learning that the Professor was not only an uncaring father but a mean one into the bargain. Oh no. He had to make it a point to disclose my plans to Uncle Quentin, as if to show the depths of my seemingly endless capacity for foolishness in trying to avenge a man not worth avenging.''

Then a small, satisfied smile lit Victoria's woebegone countenance, as she remembered her uncle's reaction once she had shown him the snuffbox and repeated for him the Professor's last words. She could actually see the light of mischief creep into his bright blue eyes as Uncle Quentin's love of adventure quickly overrode the little bit of good sense the passing of the years had granted him.

''You'd have to go about in Society if you wanted to catch the murderer,'' Quentin had pointed out, still holding the snuffbox in one pudgy hand and lifting it to the light, the better to see the workmanship of the script engraving on its lid. ''The Season's already started but, given enough money—which, as I figure it, is where I come in—I see no reason why we can't have you rigged out in fine style in time for you to hobnob with the lords and ladies at most of the festivities. Right, Willie?''

Victoria's smile faded as she remembered the battle

that had taken place once Willie had entered the room to immediately put forth objections to Quentin's outlandish suggestion. "The girl's in mourning, you overstuffed dolt!" she had protested hotly, earning for herself naught but an amused chuckle and an "As if anyone gives a fig for dead professors these days," before Quentin demanded paper and pen be brought to him posthaste so that he could start making a list of every last item that was necessary for a "prime come-out, slap up to the echo or I'm a Dutchman!"

Her temples pounding, Victoria had taken refuge in the glass that her uncle had already refilled twice, drinking deeply until she chanced to look up and realized that Willie had somehow grown an extra head. Carefully setting her glass down on a side table, she had closed her eyes and counted to ten, opening them to find that, while the housekeeper's anatomy had returned to normal, her own stomach was beginning to feel decidedly unbalanced.

When Quentin had stopped for breath—he had been chattering nineteen to the dozen about ball gowns and modistes and jewelers, knowing that Wilhelmina would be hard-pressed to withhold her approval of anything that would serve to improve her dear Victoria's position in the world—Victoria had said thickly (for her tongue seemed to have grown two sizes in her mouth), "I doubt I'll take in Society."

And that, Victoria remembered now as she buried her face in her pillow, was when her dearest Wilhelmina and her newly discovered uncle had turned on her as one, united in their resolution to not only present Victoria to Society, but to make her its queen.

"Fresh air and vegetables," Wilhelmina had pronounced importantly, crossing her arms across her ample bosom as she looked to Quentin for confirmation.

"And red meat," Quentin had added, nodding his head in the affirmative. "And plenty of cow's milk. I'll have a cow brought to the door every morning. You can do that, you know, if you have the blunt."

"We'll have to do somethin' with that hair," the housekeeper had gone on, her eyes narrowing as she assessed her mistress. "There's just too much of it. Quentin, do you think you could—"

"Done!" he had promised warmly. "Then the child needs rigging out from head to toe. Burn everything she owns, Willie my dear, and—"

"Stop it!" Victoria remembered she had then screeched hysterically, clapping her hands to her ears as she had run from the room to hide in her chamber, where she still lay, desperately trying to discover some small bit of sanity still remaining in a world suddenly run mad.

"How I loathe and detest that odious Patrick Sherbourne!" she said fervently into the darkness surrounding her bed. "This is all his fault. Willie and Uncle Quentin will push me...and prod me...and dress me up like—like a plum pudding—and then push me into Society, just so people like Wickford can giggle up their sleeves at someone like me, the veriest nobody, trying to peacock about like I belong there. How on earth will I ever bear it?"

Her outburst over, Victoria took several deep breaths and closed her eyes, intent on taking refuge, at least for a little while, in sleep. But her eyes opened wide as yet another horrible thought invaded her weary brain. Sitting up straight in her bed once more, she wailed, "My spectacles! What does it matter how I shall *bear* Society? Since I absolutely refuse to wear my horrid spectacles in public, what is more to the point is—how will I ever *see* it!''

CHAPTER NINE

"HAVE ANOTHER ONE of those muffins, Missy, and be sure to put a dollop or two of that nice honey Quentin brought home on top. And drink up all your milk," Wilhelmina prodded as she slipped a warmed plate holding two rashers of thick bacon in front of her mistress. "Your Uncle Quentin's payin' a pretty penny for it, you know."

Waiting only until she had chewed her piece of buttered toast sufficiently in order to swallow it without choking, Victoria complained, as she had at every meal for the past two weeks. "Couldn't you at least be a little more subtle, Willie? I feel like I'm being fattened up for Christmas dinner."

The housekeeper only sniffed dismissively, while covertly edging the muffin dish closer to Victoria's elbow. "Don't be silly, Missy."

"Silly, is it?" Victoria exclaimed. "I've already gained so much weight that none of my gowns feel comfortable, and still you and Uncle Quentin persist in force feeding me hourly from dawn till midnight. Confess, Willie, Uncle's out in the back garden right now, sharpening his axe. Do you plan to serve me up with an apple in my mouth? Heaven knows I've already been stuffed."

"Here now, Puddin', is that any way to talk to my poor, darling Willie?" Quentin Quinton admonished fondly as he entered the room, stopping only to ruffle

the short cap of dark brown curls that were all that remained of Victoria's long tresses before snatching up a
warm muffin and lowering his ample form into a chair.

"Dear Uncle," Victoria admonished after giving out
a long-suffering sigh, "if you would please desist in addressing me by that ridiculous appellation, I should be
most sincerely grateful."

Quentin wrinkled up his snub nose and turned to Wilhelmina for assistance. "Apple...what? What did she
say, dearest? I love the little girl more than I can say—
after all, she's m'only living relative—but I'll be dashed
if I can understand her worth a groat when she starts in
to spouting those jawbreaking words."

Wilhelmina paused in the act of clearing away the
empty egg platter long enough to notice that Quentin
had poured honey all over his muffin and was now in
danger of dribbling some of the sweet confection onto
his cravat. Snatching up a large white linen serviette, she
began tucking it firmly around his neck as she informed
him sharply, "Miss Victoria says to stop calling her Puddin', just like I keep tellin' you to leave off callin' me
dearest. I'm not your dearest, and I haven't been for
more than twenty years. Here now, lift that mess of chins
you call a neck and let me stuff this down under your
collar."

Quentin leaned forward in his chair to give Victoria
a broad wink. "She's crazy with love for me, Puddin';
always has been." Then, looking up at Wilhelmina,
whose cheeks had turned bright pink as she realized
what she had just done—being so familiar with the mas-
ter of the house, even if he had been her childhood
sweetheart—he smiled and said, "That's real Dresden
lace on m'cuffs too, my dearest. Perhaps you'd like to
have a go at tucking them up too?"

Prudently putting a hand to her mouth to hide her smile, Victoria shook her head, still able to marvel at the easy way Quentin had of disconcerting the usually unflappable Wilhelmina. In the two weeks since Quentin Quinton had moved his considerable baggage into the Professor's old bedroom, the one-time sweethearts had kept up a running battle—most of the skirmishes ending with the housekeeper fleeing the room in confusion.

Wilhelmina may have called Quentin a randy old goat when he snuck up behind her to deliver a quick pinch to her ample bottom, but Victoria could not help noticing that the woman had been taking even more than her usual care with her appearance of late, arranging her beautiful hair in a most becoming style—her white aprons starched and pressed to within an inch of their lives—while her accelerated housecleaning had more than once reduced the kitchen maid to tears.

Then there was the matter of their meals, expanded in quality and quantity since his arrival, but also predominantly comprised of Quentin's favorite foods, personally prepared by the housekeeper herself. The large bowls of succulent sweetmeats—Quentin's particular favorites— that now sat on tables in nearly every room also gave mute proof to Wilhelmina's true feelings about the man who had deserted her all those years ago.

If these changes had been all that had occurred since she first discovered she had chanced to acquire a wealthy uncle, Victoria would have been a happy woman; watching Wilhelmina's courting had proved to be most amusing. But, as she already knew to her great despair, this was not the only change to have taken place in the tall, narrow house on Ablemarle Street.

Victoria had spent the last fortnight being stuck with pins jabbed at her by a small army of seamstresses, attacked by a scissors-wielding Frenchman with a heavy scent of garlic on his breath, marched up and down the narrow drawing room by a red-faced, puffing Italian dance-master who stood a full foot shorter than she, and drilled in the proper way to curtsy to a countess by a wizened old crone who had the best breeding, the smallest pension, and the least teeth of anyone Victoria had ever encountered.

Victoria crawled into bed every evening, exhausted, to dream of milliners and modistes and glovers, all pursuing her down dark alleyways, trying their best to catch her and measure every inch of her, from her nearly denuded head to her ludicrously painted toes, only to wake in the morning in time to face another day packed with unending struggles to maintain some control over her own body.

Now, looking down at the carefully sculpted nails on the tips of fingers that had been dipped into cucumber juice and massaged with crushed strawberries and cream until the ink stains had faded and the calluses had disappeared, Victoria wished yet again that she had had the good sense to deny even so much as ever *thinking* about discovering the identity of the Professor's murderer.

There were, she admitted to herself, certain things about her new situation that appealed to her, such as her twice daily airings in the small park nearby and the soft, silky feel of her new undergarments. But no matter how much of his vast fortune Uncle Quentin was willing to pour into the eager, waiting hands of London's merchants—and it appeared that his bounty, as well as his purse, was extremely generous—Victoria knew that mere window dressing was not enough to have her accepted with open arms by the *ton*.

Her background was unexceptionable enough, with no smell of the shop clinging to her, and once word of the ridiculously extravagant dowry Quentin had settled on her got round, Victoria was sure she would find at least a few invitations thrown her way; but she was likewise convinced that none of these invitations would put her within a hundred miles of any social gathering frequented by such exalted personages as the Earl of Wickford or Mr. Pierre Standish, her two most likely suspects.

Victoria bit down sharply on another thick piece of bacon as the thought of Patrick Sherbourne engendered in her a swift desire to indulge in some sort of physical exertion, and since Wilhelmina had threatened dire consequences if her young mistress were even to entertain the thought of lifting a finger to help with any domestic chores, chewing seemed to be the most exercise she was allowed.

How that infuriating man would chortle with glee if he could see Miss Victoria Quinton now—sitting politely at table, her elbows pressed primly at her sides, quietly partaking of her breakfast while her wayward uncle and optimistic housekeeper planned the social coup of the Season—Victoria thought helplessly, unable any longer to fight the urge to allow her shoulders to droop.

"Sit up straight!" Wilhelmina barked, sergeantlike, picking up immediately on Victoria's lapse. "Being tall is nothin' to be ashamed of, you know."

"Don't you know that even you can't fashion a silk purse out of a sow's ear?" Victoria responded somewhat lamely, pushing her shoulders back against the hard chair, for she had just graduated from the uncomfortable backboard the day before and could only hope the housekeeper wouldn't see fit to strap it back on her for her sins. "Besides, Willie, everyone knows Incomparables are always small, blonde, and dainty." And pretty, she added to herself.

"That, Puddin', was last year," Quentin told her bracingly. "This year there's to be something new for the gentlemen to wax poetic over, a tall, dark-haired beauty who's going to set this town on its ear!"

Victoria looked across the breakfast table at her uncle—sitting back in his chair, his thumbs hooked on the pockets of his pink satin waistcoat—sighed, and slowly shook her head. "I appreciate all that you're attempting to accomplish, Uncle Quentin, truly I do, and I'm overcome by your condescension. But it's plain as a pikestaff that I am not cut out for the social whirl. Why, I don't even have a female chaperone! Why don't we just stop now, before you waste any more money on such a wild scheme."

Quentin Quinton had the sort of round, cherubic face that could, when he applied himself, assume a sorrowful expression capable of wresting tears from a stone. Taking a deep, shuddering breath, he conjured up just such an expression now, seemingly suppressing a sob as he lamented, "That's it, then? You'd give up the quest just like that, at the first piddling roadblock? I had thought you had more of your mother in you, Puddin', really I did."

Victoria felt as if she had just kicked a kitten. Looking from her crestfallen uncle to the long-suffering expression now evident on Wilhelmina's face, she knew she was defeated. She had spent the past two weeks fighting every change, balking at every new gown or dancing lesson, but the time had passed for turning craven. She was committed to carrying out what had been—before Quentin arrived on the scene—only a wild, improbable flight of fancy. "Oh, all right!" she conceded grimly. "You may both take those tragedy queen looks off your faces. I have uttered my last objection."

"Then we may feel free to get on with it?" Quentin murmured artfully, not about to relinquish his woeful expression until he was sure he had gained a total victory.

"You are free to indulge yourselves to the top of your bents, both of you," Victoria declared fatalistically. "But I warn you—I am not so blind that I don't know that you have more than one reason for launching me into Society. Just don't go reserving St. Paul's for the wedding, if you please. Remember, it's a murderer we're after, and not a husband."

"A husband?" Wilhelmina repeated blankly, her eyes opened wide in innocence. "Quentin, did you hear that? Wherever did the girl get that silly idea? As if we'd ever let such a wild thought enter our heads."

"Not us, dearest, eh?" Quentin concurred, placidly reaching for a piece of bacon. "We know Puddin' would give us short shrift if ever we tried to play Cupid or some such thing. Besides, I thought we agreed; it's m'poor brother's death we're out to avenge, heaven rest his soul." Raising his eyes to heaven, he then moved his lips as if in silent prayer.

Unable to watch this farce with a straight face any longer, Victoria picked up a muffin and lightly tossed it in her uncle's direction. Laughing, she scolded, "You two really bear off the palm, do you know that?"

Deftly catching the muffin, Quentin nodded to acknowledge this faint praise. "Pass the honey pot, Puddin', since it looks like you've taken over the serving this morning. Willie, my love, why don't you sit down and rest yourself a bit after fixing us this fine repast?

There's enough here to feed a regiment. Repast," he repeated then, holding his knife up in front of him to admire its carved hilt. "I learned that word from a gentleman I met in Bombay. Secretary to a duke, he was, until he ran off with the Duke's money box. Lovely man. I learned a lot from him."

Wilhelmina looked nervously around the room, as if she expected the Professor to burst in at any moment to order her back to the kitchens before throwing Quentin out on his ear. "I really shouldn't—"

"Oh, don't talk fustian, Willie," Victoria pleaded, hopping up to pull out a chair for the housekeeper. "You're family."

Raising a hand to pat at the large knot of hair that lay at the base of her neck, Wilhelmina colored prettily, then sat down, a coquettish smile lighting her features. "Oh, isn't this grand!" she said, then giggled.

"Uncle," Victoria said, suddenly feeling inspired, "couldn't we get Willie a new wardrobe, and some lessons too? Then she could be my chaperone. I'd certainly feel less alone if I had Willie by my side when I went about town."

Quentin looked over at Wilhelmina, who had jumped to her feet the moment she had heard Victoria's suggestion, her usually pink complexion now suddenly chalk-white, and could not suppress a shout of laughter. "My Willie out in Society? Lord, Puddin', why do you think she wouldn't leave with me all those years ago?"

"But—" Victoria protested, worrying that Wilhelmina might be insulted by his words.

"No," he pushed on, unheeding, "my Willie has no love of adventure in her heart, and the thought of sitting in some titled lady's parlor with a turban stuck on her head would be enough to send her scurrying right back to the country to hide her head in a haystack.''

"He's right, Missy," the housekeeper agreed, hanging her head. "I never was the one for gaddin' about."

"Besides, I've already found a chaperone for you, and a right proper young woman at that," Quinton announced, gaining Victoria's undivided attention. "She'll be here within the week, if I read her letter right. She answered my advertisement in the newspapers, you know. Pretty handwriting. Puddin', do you really spell Saturday with two *T*'s?"

"Only one *T*, Uncle," Victoria informed him straight-faced. "But it's a common mistake."

"I thought so," Quentin said, looking a bit relieved. "She forgot the *E* too."

Victoria opened her mouth, thought better of what she was about to say, and asked for another piece of bacon.

Wilhelmina, still unsure whether to be relieved by Quentin's attempt at rescue or indignant over his low opinion of her courage, mustered enough spirit to sniff disparagingly at his description of the woman he had hired. "Chaperone, you say. That girl didn't sound to be more than eight and twenty herself, even if she is a widow. More like a companion, I'd say, and even then the tongues are sure to wag when the two of them go about together of an evening."

A young woman? More of a companion than a chaperone? Victoria felt her heart skip a beat as she thought of how lovely it would be to be able to converse with someone nearer her own age. She had never had a real friend—someone who might be able to answer some of the questions that had been plaguing her ever since she first set sight on Patrick Sherbourne and felt some strange stirrings deep inside her that she would rather die than mention to Wilhelmina. "What's her name, Uncle, this companion you have secured for me?"

"Emma," Quentin told her, then added almost under his breath, "Emma Hamilton."

CHAPTER TEN

"I KNOW IT IS a *vastly* unfortunate name," the incredibly small, blonde-haired beauty apologized in her soft voice a week later as she sat in the Quinton drawing room, "but as I loved Harry dearly, it couldn't be helped. I do hope it won't cause you any undue embarrassment."

Victoria, who had been sitting across from her newly arrived companion—feeling taller and darker and homelier by the minute—could only shake her head and continue to stare at the fragile doll who was looking at her out of the widest, clearest blue eyes she had ever seen.

"Mama, bless her soul, for she has been gone these past seven years, used to say that I should have called myself Emma Connington-Hamilton, just to avoid confusion, you know, but I didn't think I could possibly do that without insulting Harry most dreadfully, don't you? I mean, after all, it wasn't as if *I* had ever danced on a tabletop for some wicked lords or draped shawls around myself and struck Attitudes for anyone who wished to see, was it?"

At last Victoria found her tongue. "Of course I don't mind about your name, Mrs. Hamilton. Only a poor-spirited person could be so cruel as to cast aspersions on you, or Lady Hamilton for that matter, as I for one believe we should thank her for making poor, brave Lord Nelson so happy in his last years. If your name offends anyone, it will only be because England should be ashamed to remember how shabbily it has treated Lady Hamilton, especially since Lord Nelson expressly asked the government to take care of her for him.''

Emma smiled sweetly, showing off her perfect white teeth. ''Oh, you are just as knowledgeable as Mr. Quinton said you were in his advertisement. Such a dear man, your uncle. How unusual for a female to know so much about matters of state. I must say I am impressed, Miss Quinton.''

Victoria, who secretly wished she knew as much about dancing on tabletops and posing in Attitudes while dressed in draperies as she did about the less romantic features of the lives of Lady Emma Hamilton and Lord Horatio Nelson, could only sigh and say, ''Please call me Victoria, Mrs. Hamilton. After all, we are going to be much in company with one another for the next few months, aren't we?''

''Oh dear, should I? I mean, you are my employer, after all, even if it is that wonderful Mr. Quinton who actually engaged my services as chaperone. Such a dear man, Mr. Quinton. Oh—I said that already, didn't I? Harry, rest his soul, always told me I should try more diligently to remember what I have said—or was it that I should be more diligent in saying only things worthy of being remembered? Ah, well,'' she concluded, folding her tiny hands daintily in her lap, ''I don't believe it matters much now, does it? And please, Victoria, you must call me Emma. Only if you wish to, of course,'' she ended in a breathless rush.

''I would like that, um, above all things!'' Victoria told the woman, lamely trying to sound more like a debutante. Victoria couldn't be certain, but she believed she was beginning to feel a headache behind her eyes. Was it possible that all Society females prattled on like Emma

Hamilton? And if they did, how could someone like Patrick Sherbourne possibly help but seek his entertainment elsewhere, with women who, because of either their background or their profession, could at least be counted on to know whether or not the sky was blue—and then be able to say so with some measure of conviction!

"When do you plan your first foray into Society, Victoria?" Emma asked then, belatedly remembering that she was in Ablemarle Street as an employee and not an invited guest. "Have you a list of invitations you wish me to go through, to help you decide which entertainments would be best suited to an innocent young lady? That's what I did for Mrs. Witherspoon last year when I acted as companion for her dear Henrietta's come-out. Such a sweet girl, Henrietta. If only she could have done something about those dreadful teeth. I wonder who's chaperoning her this year."

Wilhelmina came into the drawing room then, intent on ushering the new chaperone upstairs and helping her unpack her belongings (just to see if the beautiful but vacant-faced young woman had any clothing more suitable to her new post than the shabby blue traveling costume that had been inexpertly darned in at least three places), saving Victoria from having to admit that she had not as yet a single card of invitation to her credit, even though Uncle Quentin had sent announcements of her debut to the newspapers over a week earlier.

Once the two women had exited the room, Victoria stood up and reluctantly walked over to the mirror, the same one she had made use of after her first insulting interview with Patrick Sherbourne. Tilting her head to one side, she carefully assessed her new, shorter hairstyle, still trying to decide if she looked like a fashionable ingenue or a slightly long-haired peach.

Thrusting out her bottom lip, she then transferred her scrutiny to the modest strip of naked flesh showing above the scooped neckline of her green-sprigged muslin morning gown, comparing her still somewhat prominent, though straight, collarbones with the cushiony expanse of skin that had peeked out above Emma Hamilton's neckline.

"I may no longer resemble a plucked chicken—thanks to Willie's hourly meals—but I still look like I have more bones than any one female should. And entirely too much neck," she added, running a hand up her throat and over her finely chiseled jaw and then back down to her chest.

"Excuse me, ma'am, but the housemaid who answered the door led me to believe I would find Miss Quinton in this room. Would it be possible for you to—*Good God!* Miss Quinton, is that really you?"

Victoria's hand froze where it was, which was why she could feel the unsettling reaction Patrick Sherbourne's deep voice immediately effected on her heartbeat. Whirling stiffly to face him, she stifled the mad impulse to cross her spread palms over her exposed neckline and forced her hands to fold themselves together lightly at her waist, hoping against hope that she presented a picture of calm assurance.

"It *is* you," the Earl said again, as if confirming his own assumption. Holding out his right hand, he advanced toward her, smiling widely. "Miss Quinton, I have to own it. Please perceive me standing before you, openmouthed with astonishment."

Immediately Victoria's back was up, for she was certain this smiling man was enjoying himself quite royally, pretending that she had overnight turned from a moulting crow into an exotic, brilliantly plumed bird.

"Oh, do be quiet," she admonished, furious at feeling herself blushing as he continued to hold his hand out to her. "If I look a complete quiz, it is all your fault—telling Uncle Quentin about my plan to ferret out the Professor's murderer. Now, if you have done amusing yourself at my expense, I suggest you take yourself off on your usual immoral pursuits, as I have more than enough on my plate without having to stand here listening to your ludicrous outpourings of astonishment."

Dropping his ignored hand to his side, Patrick merely smiled all the more as he unabashedly quipped, "Oh dear, how distressing. Now you've gone and done it, Miss Quinton. Just as I was about to search out your uncle and kiss him on both cheeks for having brought about a near miraculous transformation, you had to go and open your mouth." He shook his head in mock sorrow. "Ruined the whole effect in the twinkling of an eye. Pity, that."

Victoria, who had not as yet had time to build up any real confidence in her new, showier appearance, perversely took comfort in Patrick's remarks. Peering across the room at him carefully—and thanking her lucky stars that her spectacles were tucked away safely in her pocket—she asked huskily, "You—you actually *like* the way I look? You don't think I look—*silly?*"

Sherbourne, whose palate had become more than a little jaded—as he had limited his indulgences to only the most sophisticated sort of female for more years than he cared to count—found himself oddly touched by Victoria's artless questions and decided to put himself out a bit for her.

Sticking his quizzing glass to his eye, he began a leisurely stroll all the way around the young woman, touching her lightly on the shoulder so that she remained fac-

ing front as she tried to turn with him (his impersonal
touch nearly turning Victoria's knees to water, had he
only known).

What he saw pleased him more than he could have
believed possible. He most especially liked the short cap
of dark brown curls that seemed somehow to soften, yet
highlight her finely boned cheeks and chin. Her curiously amber eyes appeared to have grown in size beneath their straight, dark brows, he realized, and how he
had ever missed noticing her wide, perfectly sculpted
mouth he could not understand.

His circuit around her completed, he stood back several paces and ran his eyes impersonally along her figure,
taking special note of her gracefully elongated throat and
extraordinary posture. She was unfashionably thin, although not unhealthily so, and the line of her bosom was
far from imposing, but for the most part he believed he
could safely say that hers was a figure that would elicit
quite a bit of envy among many of the overly cushioned
debutantes now in circulation—not that he would ever
dare to voice that particular opinion to Victoria. After
all, he valued his life!

Finally, just as Victoria thought she would not be able
to stand still another moment, the Earl allowed his glass
to drop and cleared his throat in order to pronounce his
conclusions. "I make you my compliments, Miss Quinton. I would not go so far as to say that you have been
transformed into an unbelievably ravishing creature, for
you have not, but I do believe you have taken great
strides since last I saw you in this room."

I will not be missish, I will not be missish, Victoria
repeated over and over in her head, trying very hard not
to cry out her disappointment at this faint praise. Instead,
swallowing down hard on her feelings, she forced a

laugh, trying to show the Earl that his opinion meant less than nothing to her.

Then, when he seemed about to expand on his conclusions, she broke in crushingly, "Thank you, sir, for that candidly expressed opinion. However, I do believe that you have overstepped the bounds of propriety in speaking so to a young woman not yet out. Therefore, I believe I find it incumbent upon myself to depress your attempts at familiarity and ask you to please leave."

Patrick raised his hands and applauded softly before declaring with maddening calm, "Well done, Miss Quinton. You have put me well and truly in my place. I commend you. Now, why don't you stop trying not to pout and be a good little girl and run to get your cloak. I, out of the goodness of my heart, have taken it upon myself to give you an airing in the park this afternoon."

Victoria looked at Sherbourne as if he had suddenly sprouted an extra head, disbelief written all over her expressive face. "Why would you want to do that?" she asked, suddenly suspicious of his motives.

"Ah, Miss Quinton, I am crushed, truly crushed," he answered sadly, shaking his handsome blond head. "Having seen your uncle's insertion in the *Morning Post* more than a week ago, I have been in danger of spraining my neck searching for you at every social gathering, but to no avail."

"You have?" Victoria breathed incredulously, her heart skipping a beat or two as she fleetingly entertained the idea that he might have been looking for her because he felt the same strange attraction that she did every time she thought of him.

"You are amazed, I know. So was I. At any rate, at long last my dullard brain realized that you had precious few acquaintances in town, a circumstance that would seem to make gaining any worthwhile invitations plague-ey difficult. Remembering your uncle with kindness, I said to myself, 'Patrick, what would a gentleman do in such a situation?' I, of course, then replied, 'A gentle-man would offer his services to the lady without de-lay'—especially when you consider that I am not with-out some reputation in this city.''

Victoria sniffed derisively, giving up any lingering notion that he saw her in any sort of romantic light. ''It is precisely that reputation which keeps me from ac-cepting your charitable offer, sir, as I harbor no secret desire to become notorious. I may not get out into So-ciety, but I too read the newspapers. Your name, like that of Mr. Standish, always seems to feature quite prominently in some of the columns.''

''Notorious? Why, Miss Quinton, I do believe I am insulted,'' Patrick replied lightheartedly. ''After all, I am considered quite the rage, you know.''

Walking across the room to sit herself down on the settee before her quaking limbs failed her completely, Victoria retorted acidly, ''*Rage,* you say, Lord Wick-ford? Yes, that word does seem to describe the reaction your presence evokes. Besides,'' she ended pettishly, ''I do not believe I should like being indebted to you in any way.''

Patrick didn't seem capable of taking the hint and go-ing away, for he merely acknowledged her insult with a nod before sitting down in the same chair he had oc-cupied on his earlier visit, seemingly settling in for a lengthy chat. ''I am boorish, of course, to remind you, Miss Quinton, but you are already indebted to me.''

''How?'' Victoria questioned dubiously. ''Surely you cannot think I owe you some sort of recompense for having set my uncle onto this mad scheme to inveigle me into Society in order to unmask the Professor's killer?''

Sherbourne pulled out his pocket watch and checked on the time, shaking his head and muttering something about keeping his horses standing too long in the breeze before answering. ''You seem to have conveniently forgotten that it is I who have so graciously allowed you to retain the Professor's collection in order to aid your amateur sleuthing, Miss Quinton. But never mind,'' he added, waving his hand dismissively, ''for it was not nice in me to remind you, was it?''

Several thoughts went flashing through Victoria's mind in the next few moments. For one thing, she hadn't had so much as a free moment in the past weeks in which to continue her perusal of the Professor's collection—which had thus far unearthed over five hundred pounds hidden randomly among its pages, and little information of any merit.

Secondly, she spared a moment to deliver a mental kick to herself for being so lax as to forget that, in some perverted way, she did owe Lord Wickford a favor in exchange for his courtesy.

And finally, although she did not linger very long on the thought, she realized that the last, the absolutely last thing she wanted was to wave goodbye to any chance of ever seeing this same Lord Wickford again.

''Yes, Miss Quinton?'' Patrick prodded wickedly, as Victoria's mouth had opened and closed several times without the young woman uttering a single sound. ''Go right ahead, my dear lady. I have been keeping count, you know, and it is your turn to insult me.''

''Why would you want to set yourself up as my knight-errant?'' she asked baldly, surprising herself as much as him with her question.

It was a good question, though, Patrick admitted to himself. Just why was he going out of his way to help this peculiar young woman? Was he becoming altruistic in his declining years? Perhaps he would soon feel himself compelled to do "good works," just as his father had done once he had enjoyed seventy years of libertine, rakehell ways, hoping against hope that turning over a new leaf would perhaps gain him his entry into heaven.

Finally, unable to come up with any answer that lent him the least satisfaction, he quipped, "One drive through the park does not constitute an act of gallantry worthy of such a title, madam. A tastefully beribboned medal for bravery perhaps, considering the fact that I shall be opening myself to listening to your less than flattering remarks about me for the length of time it will take me to introduce you to a few of the more influential hostesses, but that is all. Now, Miss Quinton, are you going to come with me or not? If my new team is left standing much longer, my groom will scold me unmercifully all the way home."

"What's this? A ride in the park? Sounds like a jolly fine idea to me, Puddin'. What are you waiting for? Go tell Willie to fetch your bonnet, and then you can be on your way—right after me and his lordship here have a little sip of something while we wait."

"Yes, Uncle Quinton," Victoria breathed fatalistically, looking up to see her uncle already heading for the decanter that now stood on the table in front of the settee. At least the final decision had been taken out of her hands—allowing her to feel she had won a small victory. "But don't talk too long, as his lordship's horses are standing in the breeze," she added, silently praying that Quentin couldn't do too much damage with his bragging tongue before she could seek out her bonnet and return to the room.

"Nonsense, Miss Quinton," Sherbourne contradicted pleasantly, already rising to his feet. "I'll just step outside and instruct my groom to walk them a bit. After all, it's been quite some time since I've had a chance to speak with your uncle. I'm sure he has much to tell me about what you've been up to since last I saw you."

"I know," Victoria conceded gloomily, heading for the door as she muttered under her breath, "and that is precisely what I'm afraid of."

CHAPTER ELEVEN

THE PARK WAS A RIOT of lush greenery and colorful spring blooms, the whole scene washed clean by an early morning shower so that it smelled delicately of fragrant flowers and warm sunshine.

It presented such a delightful picture that it could only be deemed a pity that Victoria's visual appreciation of this beauty was limited to a range of slightly less than twenty-five feet in any direction.

Beyond that point, everything appeared to her as a sort of vague greenish mist below and even vaguer bluish mist above, although she wasn't about to admit that to the man sitting up beside her in the dashing vehicle she was convinced had been expressly designed by some perverse devil who knew about her unreasoning fear of high places.

So it was that—chary of confiding in anyone, and most especially the Earl, who she was sure would roast her unmercifully if he discovered her shortsightedness—she had spent the past ten minutes politely looking in any direction Patrick Sherbourne indicated, striving earnestly to comment intelligently on each one as he graciously pointed out the most interesting of the many buildings, monuments, and personages of merit they had passed along the way.

"Oh, do look over this way, Miss Quinton," Patrick was saying now, after they had been in the park only a few moments. "Why, I do believe it's Lord Storm exercising that extraordinary bit of blood and bone near the fringe of the park. Yes, yes, that's who it is all right, and there's the Duke of Avonall and his marvelously outspoken grandmother, the Dowager Duchess, over to our left, driving in that magnificent dark blue landaulet."

Victoria obligingly turned in the direction he was indicating, truly wishing she could see these intriguing sights, and squinted hopefully into the distance, eventually singling out a largish blue blob that she believed to contain the famous Duke and the Dowager Duchess. "I thought I had read somewhere that the Duke was taller," she commented, leaning forward a bit in the hope her eyes would focus better that way.

"He's sitting down, Miss Quinton," Patrick put in unnecessarily, trying hard not to smile as Victoria stared intently at the equipage he had pointed out—the one containing the immense person of Mrs. Imogene Throgmorton and her constant companion, her beloved sheepdog, Hercules.

The chit can't see more than an inch beyond the tip of her nose, he thought in amusement, though he was sure she would rather die than admit it. For all her protestations to the contrary and all her efforts to impress me with her disdain for the foibles of Society, she is just as vain as the rest of her species. Like asking my opinion of her new appearance earlier—a question that must have cost her pride dearly—it just goes to show that all women, plain or beautiful, have the same desire to be accepted, even admired, by the opposite sex.

Stealing a look out of the corners of his eyes, he inspected Victoria's profile—or at least as much of it as he could see, thanks to the sloping brim of her attractive bonnet—and decided that her face was really quite provocative. Piquant—that was the word he had been searching for ever since he had stumbled upon her intently inspecting herself in the drawing room mirror. Piquant, and rather endearing in a strange, unsettling sort of way.

Watch yourself, Sherbourne, he warned himself silently, realizing that he was beginning to actually like this bright blue spinster with the poker-straight posture and the soft, unfocused amber eyes.

Puddin', her uncle had called her, an endearment that conjured up feelings of warmth and comfort and sweet deliciousness—hardly an apt description of the atrociously clad young woman who had only recently spared no effort in accusing him of being a possible murderer! Surely a change of hairdo and a new gown couldn't make that much of a difference in the girl.

"Does the Prince Regent often take the air in this park?" Victoria asked now, having tired of pretending an interest in the occupants of the blue vehicle which had passed nearly out of sight anyway—or at least she thought so.

"Not really," Patrick answered silkily, promptly giving in to the imp of mischief that had invaded him the moment he realized his thoughts had been taking him in a direction that did not suit his vision of himself as a carefree man about town. "But if by some chance his vehicle should happen by while we are here, I'll be sure to point him out to you. Even you couldn't miss 'His Royal Immenseness'."

Victoria's eyes snapped brilliantly as she whirled to face him, demanding, "And what is that last remark supposed to mean, sir?"

"It means, Miss Quinton," he responded jovially, "that you are as blind as the proverbial bat. Please, madam, end my suspense. Do you wear spectacles, or have you merely accustomed yourself to bumping into things? No, wait, I believe I have it—you have memorized the positioning of the furniture in your house, down to the last plant stand and footstool. Of course, it's that superior mind of yours. No wonder I didn't suspect anything earlier. My, what an enterprising young woman you are, to be sure.''

"If you are quite done?" Victoria inquired repressively before bracing herself to do battle and exploding indignantly, "I knew you were no gentleman! My eyesight is none of your concern, and certainly not open to discussion."

Patrick looked at Victoria as she sat stiffly beside him, clearly incensed at his audacity in pointing out what seemed to her to be a serious flaw, felt an involuntary twinge of pity for having amused himself at her expense, and then firmly quashed it with his next words. "Here now, Miss Quinton, don't climb up onto your high ropes on me, for after all, it was not I who mistook a dog for a duke."

Victoria turned once more on the seat to confront her tormentor. "I did *what?* Ohhh, you knew all along that I can't see clearly at any distance and you—you deliberately encouraged me to make a complete fool of myself.'' Twin flags of color flew brightly into Victoria's cheeks as she unwittingly showed the Earl more animation in that moment than she had at any time since they had first met.

"Yes," he admitted blithely (for he was, in truth, rather pleased with himself), his laughing eyes sparkling like black diamonds. "I did, didn't I? I really am quite a dreadful person, just as you thought."

Suddenly, unbidden, Victoria began to see the humor

in the situation. Her chin wobbling a bit as she fought to withhold her amusement, she could only ask weakly, "Was—was it really a *dog?*"

"A rather large, shaggy sheepdog, actually," Patrick informed her, desperately striving to keep a rein on his dignity. "His, er, his name is *Her—Hercules!*" he added in a rush, just before his sense of the ridiculous got the better of him and he laughed aloud.

Victoria pressed one gloved hand to her mouth, trying with all her might to maintain some semblance of sanity in the midst of this totally insane conversation, but her efforts were without success. "His honor, the Duke of Hercules!" she could only gurgle incredulously, giving up the effort and dissolving into giggles—possibly the first spontaneous display of amusement she had shown since her nursery days.

When at last their shared laughter had trickled away, they looked at each other and smiled warily, aware of having established a sort of wary truce between them at long last. As if to test this new, fledgling friendship, Patrick, his expression sobering somewhat, leaned forward confidentially and said, "You know, being short-sighted is not something to be ashamed of, Miss Quinton. Everyone has something about themselves that they would rather not advertise to the world, but physical limitations or oddities really have very little to do with the worth of a person in the long run."

"It's very kind in you to say so, sir," Victoria began, finding the subject of her shortsightedness uncomfortable, "but then how many debutantes have you seen going down the dance in spectacles?"

"You have missed the point entirely, as usual," he said sadly, shaking his head. "Why, look at Lord Byron, for example. For Lord's sake, the man has a clubfoot—

if you will forgive my ungentlemanly reference to a portion of the human anatomy. But does that stop him from being the toast of London? No, madam, it does not, and a clubfoot is far more evident than a pair of spectacles!''

Lifting her chin slightly as she turned front once more, Victoria said tightly, ''You think I'm being foolish, don't you? Foolish, and horribly vain.''

''If the slipper fits—''

''But I can't help it! Don't you understand? I know I'm no beauty, even you said so. I shall be nervous enough just attending the theatre, or some rout party. I simply cannot conceive going into Society with an unsightly pair of spectacles stuck to my nose!''

Sherbourne nodded, seeming to accept her words as he pulled his vehicle out of the line of carriages and drew the horses to a stop. ''All right,'' he conceded equably enough, ''if you insist. In that case, however, I must tell you that, because of my admiration for your extreme courage in trying to ferret out the Professor's murderer, I feel it only fitting to volunteer my services whenever you go into company. After all, it wouldn't do to have this Society you seem to hold in such awe observe you trying to engage in an uplifting discussion with some potted plant, now would it?''

The park suddenly seemed to be cloaked in a vivid red haze as Victoria lost her temper in that complete, heedless way only those who are usually even-tempered can do. Her coldly glittering amber eyes narrowed dangerously as she moved her face closer to Sherbourne's, and she spoke her next words through clenched teeth: ''You're enjoying this, aren't you, every horrid, humiliating moment of it?''

''No, I—''

"Don't try to deny it!" she riposted swiftly, shutting him off. "This is just some sort of twisted game your type indulges in, playing with people as if they are puppets, making them dance on strings for your edification."

"Miss Quinton, please," Sherbourne interrupted, "you are in danger of becoming overwrought. I—"

But Victoria was beyond heeding. Angrily waving his words away, she continued in a fierce undertone, "Well, let me tell you, Lord High and Mighty Earl of Wickford, I shall have none of it! It was bad enough that you thought to amuse yourself at my expense, taking me out for a ride in the park just to poke fun at me, proving yet again what I already know—that I have been spinning daydreams in believing I should ever be able to enter Society in any but the most elementary way. But when you—"

"I did not," Patrick objected when Victoria stopped momentarily for breath. "Well, maybe I did—a bit—but I really didn't mean any harm, honestly. Please, Miss Quinton, if you would but let me get a word in edgewise—"

"No, I won't," Victoria answered belligerently. "You don't deserve it. As I said, I can live with what you have tried to do to me. After all, my hopes were not all that high in the first place. But I will *not* have you raising Uncle Quentin's hopes by volunteering to present me to Society. That dear man has a heart of gold, which is the only reason I have allowed him to dress me up like some Christmas pudding and try to launch me as if I really were somebody worthy of presentation. To raise his expectations the way you have by showing up in Ablemarle Street this afternoon and treating him like some bosom beau, just to dash them all at the end—why, I think it is the most deceitful, odious thing anyone has ever done!''

"Hav-ing a spot of trou-ble are you, Wick-ford?" a smoothly drawling masculine voice asked, stopping Patrick from indulging in what was his fondest desire at that moment—kissing the infuriating Miss Victoria Quinton square on her pouting full lips until she was too limp with passion to utter another word.

Shaking his head at the sound of the man's voice, both to bring himself back to reality and to rid his mind of the unsettling knowledge that he had been sitting in his high perch phaeton in the middle of the park, seriously considering making an utter fool of himself over an ungrateful, insulting—and not even very pretty—young woman who loathed the very air he breathed, he turned to greet George Brummell with almost unbelievable geniality. "Beau, my good friend! I didn't know you were back in town. It's so good to see you again. How is His Royal Highness? Is he with you?"

"Hard-ly, Patrick," Brummell replied in his usual languid way. "His Royal High-ness is still rus-ti-cating with *Mistress* Fitzherbert, I believe," he added, employing his usual derogatory way of referring to the Regent's long-standing companion, which was rumored to be one of the reasons the Beau had at last fallen out of favor with the royal personage. "But, my dear man, you are being sad-ly remiss. Must I beg?"

Sherbourne frowned a moment, still somewhat caught up in his feelings about the woman sitting so very still beside him, and unable to quickly understand that the Beau was asking for an introduction. "Oh, pardon me, George, I implore you. Please allow me to introduce my companion. Miss Victoria Quinton, may I present Mr. George Brummell?"

Beau, who had been standing in the path beside the halted vehicle, raised his hat and politely inclined his head. "Charmed, I am sure," he said smoothly, then mused, "Quin-ton, Quin-ton. Patrick I do believe you have been hiding this de-light-ful crea-ture from me, for I do not re-call the name."

Victoria, who had now had ample time to regret her recent unladylike outburst, if not the sentiments she had expressed, could think of nothing but returning to Able-marle Street as soon as possible and forgetting about the entire afternoon. She would then somehow convince her uncle that she was not suited for Society and, if neces- sary, invent some exotic illness that would keep her from ever leaving her room until the Season was over.

The man now standing before her, the famous Beau Brummell—and a person she should be trying to impress above all others—now seemed to be nothing more than an impediment to her plans. Therefore, never stopping to think about what she was saying, she merely returned his nod and told him flatly, "There is no reason to apol- ogize for not recognizing my name, Mr. Brummell, as I am nobody at all, and entirely beneath your notice."

Patrick could only watch in amazement as Brummell's finely arched left eyebrow climbed ridiculously high on his forehead, signaling his astonishment. Now she's gone and done it, the Earl thought, wincing. Nothing like insulting the most influential man in all of England to set your toes straight on the path to social ruin, even if the fellow is slightly out of favor at the moment. Rush- ing into speech before the Beau could deliver one of his blighting snubs, he said hopefully, "Miss Quinton is so endearingly modest, isn't she, George?"

"Mod-est?" the Beau repeated coldly, seemingly sur- prised. "I think not, Patrick. I should instead call it immense-ly re-freshing. Of course Miss Quinton is no-body. Af-ter all, my dear boy, she heard me say I did not know her. *No*-body is *any*-body until *I* know them. However, my dear, candid lady, I do believe I shall make it my par-tic-u-lar proj-ect to in-tro-duce you. Will that suit, Patrick?''

Sherbourne smiled knowingly, realizing that Brummell had somehow decided to champion Miss Quinton in some sort of revenge against the Regent. After all, if George could take the unexceptional Victoria Quinton and turn her into the Success of the Season, it would be a sharp slap in the face for his former benefactor, who had openly prophesied that Brummell would soon realize his folly and come crawling back to him to apologize for his recent irreverent behavior.

''If you wish it, George,'' Patrick conceded cheerfully, ''you could make my sainted great-grandmother into the rage, and the dear woman's been underground these twenty years.''

''Pre-cisely, my dear boy, pre-cisely,'' the Beau confirmed shortly, already bored with the subject and longing to be on his way. ''But I must toddle off now, as I am weary un-to death, having spent last eve-ning on the road. The scoun-drel-ly landlord had the au-dac-i-ty to put me in a room with a *damp* stran-ger. I vow I did not sleep a wink all night.''

As Patrick and Victoria watched the exquisitely dressed man walk away, nodding and bowing to every-one he passed, regally accepting their patronage as his right, Sherbourne muttered under his breath: ''That was quite a coup, Miss Quinton. Beau can be quite an ugly customer, you know. If he takes it into his head to de-stroy somebody, they may as well sell up all their belongings and head for the Colonies, for nothing will save them.''

Victoria was still watching the Beau's progress, impressed in spite of herself, and just a little bit encouraged about her chances of moving about in Society without making a complete fool of herself. Forgetting for a moment that she was not really speaking to him, she said to Sherbourne, ''Mr. Brummell seemed to like me well enough, I believe. Perhaps he was amused by what I said to him. What do you think?''

Patrick once again found himself laughing out loud, causing the slight smile Victoria had been wearing to slowly slide from her face. ''You mean that witty repartee you dazzled the Beau with, Miss Quinton? That 'I am nobody' drivel? Dear lady, please,'' he entreated earnestly as he set his team in motion, ''I beg you. Whatever else you may attempt in this Season, please, *please*, do not entertain any notion of setting yourself up as a *wit!*''

CHAPTER TWELVE

DROPPING HEAVILY into a leather wing chair at White's, Patrick gratefully accepted a glass of wine from his friend Pierre Standish and drank its contents down in one long gulp. "I squired Miss Quinton around the park this afternoon," he then said by way of explanation when he saw the politely curious look on his friend's face at his action.

"How very enterprising of you, my dearest," Pierre responded levelly, absently stroking the scar on his left cheekbone. "Was your team unusually fractious, then? You seem quite fatigued."

"On the contrary, it was Miss Quinton who was being refractory, my friend, as is her custom," Sherbourne clarified, pouring himself another glassful. "I believed myself to be performing an altruistic act, and she all but boxed my ears for my pains. I tell you, Pierre, I don't think the woman is fully furnished in her upper rooms."

Pierre lifted his chin and lightly stroked his neck above his exquisitely crafted cravat, looking at Patrick from beneath his lowered eyelids. "One can only marvel at the fact that you persist in your attentions to the lady. Her looks have improved from unbearable to vaguely tolerable since the uncle's advent onto the scene—my valet, Duvall, frequents the park she walks in, you know—but really, darling, have you honestly convinced yourself that the monstrous dowry he bestowed on the chit will keep you warm at night—or do you plan a marriage of convenience only?''

Patrick's head came up like a shot. ''Marriage?'' he protested, aghast. ''Whoever is speaking of marriage? Good God, man, how long have you been sitting here, if you have drunk enough to even consider such a thing? Besides,'' he added, narrowing his eyes slightly, ''how does it happen that you know so much about Miss Quinton and her uncle? As far as I know, her outing with me this afternoon constituted her first public appearance. And this business about a dowry—really, Pierre, there are times when I actually believe you begin to frighten me.''

Lowering his hand to press it lightly against his waistcoat, Standish dropped his chin slightly and winked at his friend. ''Ah, my love, you are not so craven. You know that I have always made it a point to keep myself informed of the activities of those in my orbit. But I am not omnipotent, alas. Tell me, does the lady in question persist in her intention to unmask her departed papa's murderer, or has she merely been swept up in the social whirl at the insistence of dearest Quentin?''

''You know Quentin Quinton?''

Making a steeple of his slim, straight fingers, Pierre then tapped them lightly against his lips as he directed a long, dispassionate stare at his companion. ''It is tactless in me to point this out, I know, but you should not answer a question with another question, my dear Patrick. In addition to bordering on the fringes of being rude, you will find that—at least where I am concerned—it is also quite an unfruitful exercise.''

There were times when Sherbourne, usually a most peaceful fellow, longed for nothing more than to square off with Pierre Standish and bang away at him until they both were bloody and spent. This, he realized as he felt his left hand clenching into a fist at his side, was one of those times.

But now, as always, he brought himself up short, remembering that this cold, seemingly deliberately arrogant, heartless man was still the same fiercely loyal Pierre Standish who had stood staunchly at his back all through those incredibly dangerous days on the Peninsula Campaign.

He was also the same caring, compassionate friend who had nursed Sherbourne back to health when his horse was shot out from under him and he had lain unconscious for three days in some vile mountain hut; the same Pierre Standish who had drunk, and wenched, and caroused with him during the rare moments the enemy had been put to rout long enough for them to indulge themselves in some sanity-restoring frolic.

Patrick knew something had happened to change Pierre into the cold, calculating man who now sat across from him; something that had occurred at Standish's country estate upon their return to England, and even their close friendship had not been strong enough to encourage Pierre to confide in him.

Patrick shifted uncomfortably in his chair, longing to lean across the table and say, "Talk to me, Pierre. Tell me why you have taken on this ruthless exterior. Do you really delight in making all around you uneasy? Who did this to you? What can I do to help?"

But he didn't, of course, knowing the fragile relationship Pierre still allowed to exist between them would disappear at that instant, leaving him with no hope of ever helping his friend.

"Silence is also considered, I believe, to be rude, my dear sir," Pierre pointed out at last, as Patrick had gotten himself lost in a brown study. "Perhaps my question was too convoluted? Allow me to simplify and rephrase it: Does Miss Quinton persist in her quest?"

Patrick took a deep breath, then nodded twice in the affirmative. "She does," he answered grimly. "The inspiration behind launching her socially comes, I believe, mostly from the uncle, although Miss Quinton seems to be swimming from one deep gravy boat to another, considering that she has just this afternoon succeeded in catching Beau's eye. He means to make her a Success. I tell you, Pierre, I don't know where this whole business will end."

"George has taken our little fledgling under his wing? Heavens, how very droll. The girl must be *aux anges*. Tell me, Patrick—does Beau realize the chit will be using *him* in order to further her investigation? My goodness, think of it, darling. Beau Brummell in the role of cat's-paw. But wait! Perhaps he too is a suspect? The mind begins to boggle."

Patrick allowed a small smile to lighten his solemn expression, as it appeared he had just achieved the impossible. *He* was about to tell Pierre something! So gratifying was the feeling that he decided to drag out the moment, pausing to call a servant over to order dinner laid for two in the dining room before pouring another glass of wine for his friend.

"I told you I took Miss Quinton out for a ride this afternoon, Pierre," he began, edging his way into the story slowly. "What I did not tell you is that I had a small, private conversation with Quentin Quinton while the lady went to fetch her bonnet and cloak. He is a delightful man, and most forthcoming."

Reaching forward to pick up his wineglass, Pierre saluted his friend before taking a sip of the dark red liquid.

"Enjoy yourself, darling, you deserve it," he drawled amicably, leaning back once more.

Patrick felt a slight flush invade his cheeks. "I didn't realize I was being so transparent, Pierre. Forgive me. At any rate, the uncle was a veritable fountain of information, believing me to be the best of good fellows since I championed him upon his arrival in Ablemarle Street, I imagine."

"Don't forget that pretty face of yours, my dearest boy," Standish slid in gracefully. "As I have told you before, it absolutely invites confidences."

"From everyone but you," Patrick, grimacing slightly, said softly before getting back to the subject at hand. "Quinton has entered into the investigation wholeheartedly since last I saw him. It seems that there is a most damning piece of evidence that Miss Quinton has unearthed, a snuffbox discovered lying near the body that fateful morning."

"Ah, not only one clue to the murderer, but two," Standish observed quietly, his finger once more going to the crescent-shaped scar. "It would appear that the man was not only violent, but untidy as well. Continue, my dear, as I am breathless to learn more."

"There were initials engraved into the lid of the snuffbox," Patrick confided in an undertone, lest someone overhear. "The letters *P* and *S,* to be precise, which leaves our dear Beau out of the running but lands both you and me at the topmost spot on Miss Quinton's list of suspects."

"Not you, dear boy," Pierre corrected lightly. "At least, not anymore, as it would seem that you have become quite the fair-haired boy in Quentin's mind's eye. A word to the wise, my darling: I do believe I was more right than I thought when I said I scented some matchmaking in the air. Best check with the lady's modiste first thing tomorrow morning—just to see if the bride clothes have been ordered.''

The room around them was becoming dim as the sunlight faded from the windows, and Patrick was forced into furious silence as a servant stopped nearby to light a brace of candles. While at first he was more than ready to jump into speech, roundly decrying Pierre's allusion to Quinton's possibly having plans for him concerning the infuriating Victoria Quinton, the Earl soon realized that he had nearly fallen for one of Pierre's oldest and best developed ploys—directing the conversation away from himself by introducing another topic that concerned him not at all.

So it was then that—when the servant, who seemed particularly inept with the tinderbox that day, finally moved away—Patrick looked levelly at his friend and said pointedly, ''Then it would seem, my friend, that you now stand alone at the head of Miss Quinton's notorious list. Unless you have some other likely suspect in mind to keep you company, now that I am found to be without sin?''

''Ah, but I do, my darling man, I most assuredly do,'' Pierre answered placidly, rising to move off toward the dining room. ''Two, as a matter of fact.''

''Two?'' Sherbourne repeated, coming to his feet to follow Standish out of the room. ''I believe I can come up with one. But can you really be thinking of our friend Mr. Spalding? No, no, my friend, not Philip. The man is a complete popinjay. He hardly has the backbone required to bash in someone's head—nor the stomach, I might add. Besides, what possible motive could he have? I doubt Philip was even acquainted with the Professor.''

''You'd rather believe I did the old boy in, then? I

call that rather poor sporting of you, darling,'' Pierre
pointed out as they sat themselves down in the dining
room.

Patrick held up his hands as if to negate his last state-
ments. ''All right, all right, you've made your point.
Philip Spalding is now officially a suspect. But who is
the second man? I've searched my brain, but I'm afraid
I've come up blank on any others with the same initials.''

With a look of disdain on his dark face, Pierre waved
away the servant offering the soup course before lifting
his knife to slice into the succulent fish that a second
hovering servant had placed swiftly before him. Only
after sampling the delicacy did he obligingly enlighten
his dinner companion. ''One Sir Perkin Seldon comes
most easily to mind, I think.''

''*Sir Perky?*'' Sherbourne exploded mirthfully. ''I'd
as lief believe *I* had done it in my sleep and failed to
remember it when I awoke. Now really, Pierre—''

''Both gentlemen,'' Pierre answered evenly, although
Patrick thought he could see a slight light of mischief
lurking in the corners of the man's eyes.

''So now we have two more suspects, in addition to
yourself, as so far the redoubtable Mr. Quinton hasn't
absolved you by the simpleminded expedient of enlisting
you in the marriage stakes. Now what? Do you plan to
sit back and watch the circus that is sure to begin once
Miss Quinton enters Society, or are you going to step
entirely out of character and take an active role in this
investigation?''

''You know me, darling. I much prefer to observe
from a safe distance. Not,'' he added languidly, ''that I
shouldn't enjoy pulling some of the strings from behind
the curtain.''

"Leaving me to take center stage, I presume," Patrick pointed out good-naturedly, resigning himself to his fate. "All right, my friend, if needs must. I shall play your little game for you, as I feel I owe you that much."

"On the contrary, my dear friend," Standish said in a curiously soft voice. "It is what *I* owe you."

If Patrick disliked Pierre's cold unemotionality since his return to London over six years ago, he now found himself even more uncomfortable with this rare display of affection. "Please don't, Pierre. After all, he wasn't such a very large Frenchman," Patrick said lightly, thinking of the soldier he had shot just as the man was about to sink his saber into Standish's back. "Now, let us get back to the matter at hand, as I find I am beginning to look forward to Miss Quinton's come-out. General Standish, your loyal subordinate awaits his first order."

"Major Standish will do, Corporal," Pierre corrected smoothly, acknowledging Sherbourne's compliment with a slight inclination of his head. "As to our plans for our suspects and the lady, why I do believe that I think it to be our duty to introduce Miss Quinton to both of them as soon as possible. Call it your Christian duty, if you will."

"How do you propose we—I shall correct myself before you do—I mean, how do you propose that *I* arrange such a meeting?"

"Why Patrick, my darling boy," Standish scolded, shaking his head, "you don't mean to tell me that I have to think of everything, do you? Isn't it enough that I, your commanding officer, have given you an assignment? Do I have to hold your hand as well while you carry it out?"

CHAPTER THIRTEEN

VICTORIA STOOD ALONE in her darkened chamber, watching from behind the sheer underdraperies as the lamplighter moved slowly down the street, leaving the yellow glow of the lamp near Number Sixty-three behind him, then vanishing into the darkness.

Twin flames of light reflected on the smooth lenses of her spectacles as she stared into the heart of the soft glow as if it were some sort of divine fire wherein she could find the answers she sought.

For there *were* questions; so many questions.

Who had killed the Professor—and why?

Even more to the point, why was she, the man's unloved daughter, going to such lengths to unmask his murderer?

"Because you promised a dying man you would do just that, that's why," she reminded herself aloud, wincing at the sound of self-mockery she heard in her voice. She sighed deeply, then reluctantly admitted the truth. "Because you wanted some small bit of excitement before you resigned yourself to spending the rest of your days steeped in the same dreary dullness that has so far marked your existence, *that's* why."

Closing her eyes, she turned away from the window. "That may be how this whole crazy scheme began," she jibed scornfully, "but even that is not the whole truth, and you know it. Admit it, Victoria, you are allowing yourself to be carried along in this mad rush into Society so that you can be close to Patrick Sherbourne. You want to watch him as he goes gracefully down the dance, perhaps snatch a moment in conversation with him so that you can drink in his beauty, breathe the same air as he, delight in his smiles, and pray for the accidental brush of his arm against yours. In short, you, my dear, have read one too many Minerva Press novels, if you actually believe such a man would ever think to fix his interest with someone such as you!''

Clapping her hands to her burning cheeks, Victoria raced over to the bed and cast herself down on it, shaken to the core now that she had finally voiced her feelings aloud. What had begun as an investigation based on cold logic and Dame Reason had—within one bewitching twinkling of Sherbourne's dark eyes that fateful day the Professor's will was read—turned into a hopelessly convoluted melodrama, complete with a stars-in-her-eyes heroine mooning in her chamber over the prerequisite unattainable male.

"And I don't even *like* the man," she muttered wretchedly into her pillow. "He treats me like a particularly unlovely, backward child—when he isn't baiting me unmercifully, that is. Why, the only reason he comes around at all is for his own twisted amusement, as if I am some freak at the fair that he delights in tormenting, just to see me perform. I should hate him, actually," she vowed with some heat, pushing out her full bottom lip in a satisfied pout.

Then, turning over onto her back so that she could stare up at the shadows dancing on the ceiling above her flickering bedside lamp, Victoria slipped off her spectacles and began chewing on one earpiece, as she had done in her childhood. She could feel a soft curl of pleasure growing deep inside her as she remembered how cherished she had felt when Patrick had taken hold of her elbow in order to help her up into his phaeton just a few hours earlier.

Of course, he had not been quite so solicitous upon their return to Ablemarle Street, but she had decided to overlook this lapse, preferring to think that he had been put slightly out of coil by Mr. Brummell's kind attentions to her while they were in the park.

As for her impulsive outburst of temper—an unfortunate circumstance which her hindsight had thankfully colored in a more lenient hue—it had not been referred to again by either of them, leading Victoria to believe she had been forgiven.

"He couldn't have just been being polite in saying that my new appearance was pleasing either, for heaven knows he can be most brutally frank when it comes to compiling lists of my shortcomings," she mused, gnawing thoughtfully on one of the earpieces of her spectacles.

"And, although he was perfectly beastly in teasing me about my shortsightedness, he did offer to assist me in public so that I don't make a complete fool of myself by tumbling into a ditch or something. That is not the action of a completely selfish man. No," she decided, a slow smile teasing her lips, "the Earl has a good heart, I am sure of it—not like that Pierre Standish, who has no feelings at all."

Rising from the bed in order to search out her nightgown—the one the efficient Willie must have returned to the cupboard after Victoria had laid it on the bed not an hour earlier—unbuttoning her gown as she went, her smile faded as she remembered the mysterious locked box the solicitor had handed Mr. Standish.

"The Earl may no longer be a suspect," she declared with conviction as her simple dimity gown whispered softly past her slim hips to gather in a soft yellow pool around her feet, "but Mr. Pierre Standish certainly fits all the requirements. If only he and Patrick were not such obvious good friends. Proving Mr. Standish to be a murderer could make things very awkward for Patrick, but if I give up my search I will likewise relinquish my only reason for being in Society at all. And *that* I refuse to do!"

This little bit of introspection brought Victoria back to thoughts of her discovery earlier in the evening of a secret compartment in the Professor's desk, although how it had remained a secret throughout Wilhelmina's twice-annual waxing and polishing, she was at a loss to understand. The contents of this compartment—a small ledger written in some sort of numbered code—had served to confirm Victoria's growing feeling of there being "something rotten in Denmark," although she had not as yet had time for a full study of the book.

"Tomorrow I shall closet myself in the library and devote my full attentions to breaking the Professor's code," she decided, walking toward her bed. "I always thought there was a darker side to the man, and now I have to discover if this darker side could be the real reason behind his murder. Indeed, I am almost beginning to feel empathy for whoever did him in. What an unnatural child I am! But," she ended on a sigh, "if the Professor was truly evil, it would go a long way in making me feel less an ungrateful daughter.

"I wonder," she added, hesitating a moment at the side of the bed. "Does Uncle Quentin have similar suspicions? And the Earl—perhaps he knows more than he is telling me, and that is why he has been so eager to lend me his assistance. This whole affair is becoming more and more curious.''

She dragged back the worn cotton bedspread and slid gratefully between the covers, wriggling about slightly until she found her usual comfortable spot in the middle of the ancient mattress. "What a complete change from my former dull life. There are so many questions now, so many problems," she complained, stifling a yawn. "I should be feeling quite put upon, actually."

She slipped her hands behind her head, stretched out her legs until the covers came free from the bottom of the bed, and wiggled her bare toes. A wide grin split her face as she realized that she was not feeling the least depressed. "Actually, I can't remember the last time I was this happy!"

CHAPTER FOURTEEN

EMMA HAMILTON WAS FITTING into her new niche in the Quinton household with the ease of someone who has through necessity made a career out of making herself as amiable and comfortable as possible.

She complimented Wilhelmina on the woman's extraordinarily efficient housekeeping (while secretly wondering if she would ever again feel it safe to leave her knitting on a chair for a moment without it being whisked away into its basket while her back was turned).

She did her best to remain neutral during the constant mealtime wars (during which Wilhelmina and Quentin constantly bombarded Victoria with pleas to clear her plate, and the young lady counterattacked by way of fiercely lowered eyebrows, deadly verbal salvos, and, just once, a well-aimed dish of stewed plums).

She pasted a polite, if slightly bemused, smile on her face whenever Quentin decided to regale her with yet another implausible tale of his adventures in India, Africa, and Southern Europe (and did not whimper even once when he minutely described his interminable seasickness on the stormy voyage back to England).

But, for the most part, what Emma Hamilton really excelled at was The Nod.

She nodded her agreement to Wilhelmina's heavy, nearly indigestible menus, designed with Victoria's still-slim frame in mind.

She nodded her enthusiasm as Quentin proudly prosed on at length that all his darling Puddin' needed was a wee bit of patina added to her polish before she surprised everyone and took the town by storm.

So dependent on others for her survival was Emma that she even bit her tongue and nodded her approval when Quentin showed her his latest surprise for Victoria—a heavy, three-inch-high diamond-encrusted pin fashioned in the shape of a *Q*, which was meant to be his present to her when she received her voucher for Almack's.

What Emma thought privately about all these things, no one knew, for no one ever bothered to ask her.

For amid the whirlwind of activity that was the Quinton household, Emma had become the single calm port in a sea ravaged by storms—nodding and knitting as Quentin entertained thoughts of renting out the entire Pulteney Hotel for a ball; patting her hankie delicately to her nose and nodding as Wilhelmina told her that Quentin Quinton was simply the shiftiest thing in nature, while reeking with the scent he had slipped into her apron pocket that morning; murmuring soft nothings and nodding as Victoria patiently explained that Society meant nothing to her, that discovering the Professor's murderer was the only reason she was allowing herself to be a party to the whole insane business going on around her.

Perhaps that was why Emma immediately became the center of everyone's attention two days after Victoria's ride in the park when she finally opened her sweet, rose-bud-pink mouth and declared loudly: "*No!* Absolutely not! I cannot, I will not, allow it!"

"But why, Emma?" Victoria asked solicitously, going over to the settee to sit down beside her companion and take the woman's hand in hers. "After all, it is not as if Uncle Quentin cannot afford it. Besides, I think you've hurt his feelings. Just look at him standing over there, his poor chins dragging on the carpet—how can you be so cruel?"

Emma obediently looked over at Quinton, who did appear to be almost comically crestfallen, and her bottom lip began to tremble. "Oh, you are all so kind, so well-intentioned—but you have no real conception of what is done and what is *just not done!*"

"Oh laws," Wilhelmina muttered under her breath, searching in one of her apron pockets for a large white handkerchief, which she held out to the whimpering woman. "Anybody would think we just told her we was goin' to sell her to a chimney sweep."

Shaking her head in silent warning, Victoria waved the housekeeper away. "You must come with me, Emma," she began bracingly. "After all, how can I attend a theatre engagement if my companion refuses to accompany me?"

Emma disengaged her hands from Victoria's and fluttered them agitatedly in her lap. "It—it's not that, Victoria, you dear, sweet girl. Of course I must accompany you to the theatre. But, good gracious, I cannot allow your uncle to purchase me a gown for the evening. I am a chaperone, not a young girl on the catch for a husband." She shook her head vehemently, setting her blonde ringlets to bouncing. "It—it just isn't *done,*" she wailed again, unable to come up with anything more to the point that she could say on the subject.

"Heyday! Is that all that's got her blubbering and whining?" Quentin cut in, utterly blind to the effect his frank words might have on someone with Emma's tender sensibilities. "Good Lord, gel, I've got more of the ready than a body could spend in five lifetimes. Who's to say me nay if I want to shower a little of it on a fine, pretty miss like you? It's not like I had designs on you, or the like, seeing as how you know it's Wilhelmina holds m'heart. How did the girl get a maggoty idea like that into her head?"

"*Ohhh…*" Emma turned to Victoria in desperation, her china-blue eyes awash with tears.

"Uncle," Victoria warned quietly, wishing the well-meaning man would take the hint and withdraw before his plain speech could throw Emma into strong hysterics.

"Now don't you go pokering up on me, Puddin'," he responded, unrepentant. "Lord Wickford sent this here invitation for you and your companion to attend the theatre tomorrow night with him and one of his fancy friends. All I say is, why shouldn't little Emma here cast out a couple of lures while you're about it? You know— get herself some new duds like the ones I got you and, who knows, maybe she'll land herself a fine fish."

"Uncle!"

"Mr. Quinton!"

"Quentin!"

Quentin looked from one to another of the three women, sensing reactions of amused indignation, extreme embarrassment, and—from the love of his life— an immediate threat to his physical person, and threw up his hands as if to say, "I give up, do what you will," then quit the room, muttering under his breath about the injustice of it all. "Try to do something nice for a body, and what do you get?" the women could hear him asking as he strode away.

"You get a piece of my mind just as soon as I catch up with you, that's what you get!" Wilhelmina called after him, shaking her fist at his retreating back. "And close the door after you, Mr. Rich Man Quinton," she ordered. "Didn't you learn anythin' in that India of yours?"

A few minutes later, after Wilhelmina had also withdrawn, taking with her the sal volatile she had employed to good effect on the wilting Emma, Victoria embarked upon a lengthy rational discourse, which ended with her at last convincing her companion that accepting a few paltry gowns and other fripperies from Quentin did not constitute a rapid descent into the role of "fallen woman."

"It is so kind of you all to even think of me," Emma gushed gratefully, still dabbing Wilhelmina's enormous hankie to the corners of her eyes. "My jointure is rather small, you know, which is why I have been forced to, ah, I mean, so I find it helpful to lend my small consequence to less socially prominent young ladies like, er, that is—"

"I know just what you mean, dear lady," Victoria interrupted kindly, "and I can only say that Uncle Quentin couldn't have chosen better when he decided to ask you to join our rather strange little band. And I most assuredly am cognizant of the fact that I am certainly not going to be an easy debutante to launch. Why, any other chaperone would have thrown up her hands within an hour of arriving in Ablemarle Street, not that I could blame her."

Anyone who had the coach fare home to Hampstead Heath, Emma corrected silently, but she did not give voice to her thoughts. "Oh no, Victoria," she protested swiftly, careful to concentrate her remarks on her charge's last statement. "You must not say so! You are rather thin, and...and *tall*, and your coloring is not what is currently in fashion, but you are really a very striking girl.''

"*Striking,* is it, Emma?" Victoria quipped, pulling a wry face. "You couldn't stretch that little fib wide enough to say *beautiful,* could you?"

"But you are not beautiful," Emma responded impulsively. "Beautiful is commonplace. You are—*different.* Yes, that's it; you're different. Your marvelous carriage, that long, slim neck, those curious amber eyes. I—I think you—oh dear, this will sound so silly, I know—but I think you have a way of *growing* on a person, Victoria."

"Rather like moss?" Victoria offered dryly, smiling a bit in spite of herself.

Emma waved her hands excitedly and pointed to Victoria's face. "There! There, you see it? There's that dimple. It's so unexpected, my dear, and should be most intriguing to a gentleman. Oh no, you must not be so hard on yourself. Your Uncle Quentin may be wishing for too much when he thinks you will become the Sensation, but you will have your share of beaux, believe me."

Victoria lowered her head so that Emma couldn't see the embarrassed blush that had crept into her cheeks. If Emma thought she was passable, perhaps she did stand just a slight chance with Patrick Sherbourne. It was a wild dream, but it was heady nonetheless.

Then, reluctantly bringing herself back to the matter at hand, she remarked honestly, "Well then, dear Emma, if I can be a moderate success, you, whose size and coloring are indeed the mode, should certainly take advantage of the opportunity Uncle Quentin has offered. After all, you told me your husband has been, er, gone for over five years. I'm sure he wouldn't mind if you enjoyed yourself.''

Coloring pretty, the older woman lowered her long eyelashes and gushed, ''Dear Harry. Oh yes, Victoria, I do believe Harry would tell me I was being silly, refusing this chance for a little excitement.''

Bless you Harry, Victoria offered silently, raising her eyes heavenward. She had been sitting in the drawing room for the past half hour listening to Emma, and she longed to retire to her chamber and think about the Earl's invitation, which had arrived just an hour earlier, setting off this entire chain of events. ''Of course,'' she agreed aloud.

''Not that I should wish to make a habit of it, you understand,'' Emma persisted, still trying to convince herself she was doing the right thing. ''I wouldn't care to be thought of as a *dashing* matron. After all, I am your chaperone. But,'' she began slowly, before ending in a rush, ''it would be the greatest good fun to have a new gown.''

Sensing her victory, Victoria reached up her hands to remove her spectacles and slipped them into the pocket of her morning gown. ''Then it's settled! We shall prevail upon Uncle Quentin to allow us to go to Bond Street directly after luncheon, and we shall both acquire stunning new gowns for the theatre. You, my dear friend, may act as my guide, as I do believe I am sufficiently 'different' already without pushing the point by wearing my spectacles out in public, don't you?''

CHAPTER FIFTEEN

"Miss Victoria and Mrs. Hamilton aren't at home, you know," Wilhelmina warned the Earl of Wickford as she held out her hands to relieve him of his curly brimmed beaver and driving gloves. "They're off to Bond Street for some fancy new duds to wear to the theatre with you tomorrow night. You're welcome to wait, but only the good Lord knows how long they'll be, what with Missy takin' such care over every blessed penny she spends of Quen—, er, Mr. Quinton's money."

"Yes, thank you, Mrs. Flint, but I'm here to see Mr. Quinton," Patrick told her, handing the housekeeper his cloak just as soon as she was done flicking at his best hat with a small wire brush she had pulled from one of her many apron pockets.

"Quen— Mr. Quinton's in the library," she said then, carefully folding the cloak before draping it neatly over her forearm. "Locks himself in there now just like Missy does. And I'm *Miss* Flint, your lordship. A spinster's a spinster, I say, and I don't need to take on any hoity-toity airs like some I could name."

Wilhelmina shook her head sadly as she led the way toward the back of the house—as if resigned to the fact that she was one of the few remaining sane souls in a world gone mad—and leaving Sherbourne to follow dutifully along in her wake, feeling as if he had just been transported back to the nursery and firmly put in his place by his nanny. "Yes, ma'am—*Miss* Flint," he declared firmly. "Anything you say, *Miss* Flint."

"Like I told Missy over and over," she said then, oblivious to his sarcasm and doggedly returning to her original theme, "the daft man spends money like a drunken sailor out on a binge anyway, so what's a few pennies more for somethin' pretty for herself?"

"Or a few pennies piddled away on a butler and some other servants?" Patrick interjected mildly, just to hear the feisty housekeeper's reaction.

Wilhelmina skidded to a halt and turned to take umbrage at such a ridiculous suggestion. "A butler? Whatever for? Whyever should we be wantin' one of them useless, stiff-as-starch bodies around here?"

Patrick shrugged his shoulders, considering his answer. "Why, for one thing, a butler could answer the door for you."

"My legs look broke to you?" Wilhelmina scoffed, taking a large cloth from her apron pocket and (as long as they were just standing in the hallway and not really doing anything anyway), giving a nearby table a quick wipe.

The Earl frowned slightly, then pursued hopefully: "A butler could take charge of helping arriving guests with their outer garments—managing the disposition of their cloaks and hats and the like."

"Like I just did?" Wilhelmina asked incredulously, looking at him piercingly as she slipped the cloth back into her apron pocket.

"Exactly, Miss Flint!"

"After this butler you're talkin' about takes these cloaks," she pursued interestedly, "what does he do with them? Don't tell me any of those high and mighty blokes I've seen struttin' down the street with their noses higher than a lamppost hang them up either, 'cause I won't believe you.''

Patrick smiled, beginning to realize how neatly he had been cornered by the woman. "No, Miss Flint, the high and mighty butler does *not* usually deign to hang up the coats. He merely turns them over to a footman."

"And *he* hangs them up?" Wilhelmina pushed, smiling a bit herself.

"Uh...sometimes," he admitted, stroking his smooth chin. "It varies, depending on the size of the staff. Let's see, he could turn them over to an underfootman, who in turn could deliver them to a housemaid, who would then—"

"Who would then hand them back to the underfootman, to hand to the footman, to hand to the butler, because the bloomin' visitors would be ready to leave by then and *calling for their duds!*" Wilhelmina ended triumphantly, causing the two of them to go off into peals of laughter.

"What's going on out here, Willie my love?" Quentin asked from the doorway to the library. "You've got no need to go flirting with the Earl now that I'm home."

"Miss Flint wasn't trifling with my affections, Quentin," Patrick assured the man, "although I must say I am tempted. We were only indulging ourselves in a little game, and your dear lady has just neatly trumped my ace."

Quentin nodded, as if Wilhelmina's victory didn't surprise him in the slightest. "Always gets the last word, my Willie. She's going to make me a real brimstone of a wife, not that I'm complaining, you understand."

"Oh, fie on you, Quentin Quinton!" the housekeeper scolded, hiding her flaming cheeks in her hands. "I never said yes to you."

"You never said no, either, if I recollect correctly," Quentin reminded her, winking broadly in Patrick's direction. "Like that grand good time we two had down at the spinney when you—"

"Don't you go throwin' my past in my teeth, Quentin Quinton!" Wilhelmina shrieked, cutting off her beloved's flow of fond reminiscence.

"Now, now," Patrick interjected, hoping to calm the waters he had inadvertently stirred.

Wilhelmina wheeled around to face the Earl. "The man thinks a wife is part kitchen stove, part bed warmer. Would *you* marry a man like that?"

Patrick's lean cheeks puffed out a bit as he started to answer, then deflated again in an audible rush of released air as he stopped to consider just how he might best attack that particular question.

"Did you ever hear such a damned obstinate woman? It's a wonder to you that I still want to wed her, isn't it?" Quentin demanded, taking Sherbourne by the shoulder and turning him about rather sharply so that Quinton could look the younger man in the eyes.

Stepping hastily back two paces, Patrick spread his arms wide as if to distance himself from the two irate people and said genially, "Don't you go putting me in the middle of it, if you please. I hereby cast myself firmly in the role of innocent bystander! Somehow you have mistaken me for some wise Solomon, which I most assuredly am not. However, the answer, as far as I can see, lies quite simply in whether or not you two love each other now as you say you did all those years ago."

"*Well of course we do!*" the two answered in belligerent unison, immediately casting the hapless Earl in the role of instigator.

Patrick grinned at the pair of them. "Well, *I* believe you! You don't have to bite my head off!"

"Oh, laws!" Wilhelmina exclaimed, aghast, before clapping a hand to her mouth, having just then realized she had been arguing with a high-class nobleman as if he were "ordinary people." Then, before anyone could stop her, she scampered quickly away to the back of the narrow house to compose herself.

Patrick lowered his arms and took a step toward Quentin, opening his mouth to apologize for upsetting Miss Flint, but Quentin forestalled him by reaching out to grab the Earl's right hand hard in his and pump it up and down vigorously.

"How can I ever thank you, son?" Quentin asked earnestly. "Willie's been avoiding me like some kind of plague ever since we found my letters to her tucked away in Quennel's desk. She didn't have to really believe that I sent for her until she saw them for herself, you understand. I think it gave her a bit of a shock to figure out that she's always been and always will be my one and only true love."

"I believe I can imagine how that knowledge could serve to unsettle a person," Patrick said dryly, trying without success to pry his hand from the other man's beefy grip.

Quentin chuckled shortly. "Knocked her for six, not to wrap it up in fine linen. Well, never mind that now, right? We'll be getting ourselves bracketed all nice and tight before the month's out, I'll wager, and we've got you to thank for it. This calls for a bottle of old Quennel's finest, damme if it doesn't!"

Leaving Sherbourne to stand by himself openmouthed in the hallway—massaging his sore right hand while he gathered his thoughts—Quentin fairly danced through the open library doorway and over to the full decanter and fine array of wineglasses set out on a silver tray on one corner of the desk.

"Here you go, my boy," Quentin said, offering the Earl a full glass as Patrick moved into the room. "Drink hearty!" he suggested before downing his own portion in one long gulp and then tossing the thin crystal goblet into the cold fireplace, where it shattered into a million needle-thin splinters. "A little trick I picked up somewhere on my travels," he informed his guest, who was observing him owlishly. "I think it has something to do with having good luck."

Patrick looked at the shards of broken crystal lying on the hearth and then back to the flamboyantly outfitted Quinton, who looked less like a man of the world and more like a delighted, oversized schoolboy than anyone he cared to think of at that moment. "Seems a capital idea to me, Quentin," he agreed, gifting the man with a slow, appreciative smile. "Here's to good luck!" he said, saluting the older man with his wineglass before draining its contents and sending it winging toward the fireplace, where it exploded in a satisfying crash.

The two men stood in companionable silence for a few moments, admiring their handiwork—Patrick privately thinking the exercise to be edifying in some strange way, although potentially quite wearing on the family crystal, and Quentin trying hard to keep a brave face once he realized there'd be the devil to pay if he couldn't clean up the mess without Wilhelmina getting wind of it—before Sherbourne cleared his throat and said in a businesslike voice: "Now tell me why you sent that note round to my town house, good sir. If I read it correctly, you believe Miss Quinton might be in some sort of danger."

Quentin immediately abandoned his role of jovial host and looked up at Sherbourne, mute appeal dulling his lively blue eyes. "It is Victoria—you're right enough about that, and about the danger too—if m'brother was half the bastard I'm beginning to think he was. It seems as if it wasn't enough for him to push poor Elizabeth's father into giving her to him in marriage, or working it so that Willie and me had our falling out. Oh yes, I suspected something havey-cavey about that business at the time, although it took Willie telling me about it last week to prove the whole of it. I tell you, son, the man was a real piece of work! Come round here behind the desk, and I'll show you what I mean."

The Earl followed silently as Quinton walked behind the large desk, pulled the top left drawer completely out, and reached a hand inside the resulting space. He heard the muted sound of a spring being released, then stepped back quickly as a section of what had appeared to be the solid base of the desk fell forward onto the floor.

"Very neat," Patrick commented, bending down to slip a hand inside the dark cavity and retrieve the slim ledger that lay inside. "Quennel's private account book, I presume?" he asked, rising to his feet and handing it to Quentin unopened.

Quinton nodded, saying, "I keep it there so as to make sure Victoria never gets her hands on it."

Patrick walked back around to the front of the desk, poured two full glasses of wine, handed one to Quinton, and then sat down in one of the uncomfortable straight-backed chairs. "What was the man dabbling in, then? Espionage?"

Taking a deep drink of his wine before answering, Quentin smiled as he quipped, "Selling secrets to Napoleon? No, it was nothing so dramatic as that. I can't

be sure, but I'd say it was blackmail Quennel dealt in—
with quite a bit of success, judging from the figures written down in this little book. After cutting his teeth so
successfully on Elizabeth's father, I guess he decided to
branch out a bit.''

"Blackmail!" Sherbourne's head was immediately
filled with a half-dozen divergent thoughts, ranging from
his final meeting with the Professor to the small wooden
box he had last seen tucked under Pierre Standish's arm.
"Keep going, Quentin," he said softly. "I'd like to hear
more. Although I believe I'd like you to start at the very
beginning with Miss Quinton's grandfather, please."

Quinton sat down heavily in his brother's chair and
spread his beringed hands on the surface of the desk, as
if bracing himself for the task ahead. "That's a long
story, my friend, and not really mine to tell," he said,
sighing. "You'll keep it mum, won't you? Willie and I
are the only ones left above ground who know the whole
of it, and Elizabeth never gave permission for Willie to
tell Victoria."

"You have my word, Quentin," Patrick vowed solemnly, looking the older man straight in the eye.

"Very well, then," Quentin returned, nodding.
"Since there's no way to dress this up in fine linen, I
might just as well come out and say it—Victoria *ain't*
Quennel's daughter. Elizabeth fell head over ears in love
with William Forester—son of the local doctor, you
know, and a fine, tall figure of a fellow—but the poor
lad died in a fall from a horse before they could be
married."

"Now why do you suppose this little bit of information serves to so gladden my heart?" Sherbourne slid in
quietly.

"I knew something about it because Quennel and I

were studying our Latin grammars in the next room when the squire came to our father for advice, seeing as how Elizabeth had told her father she was breeding. Papa was the vicar, you'll recall. A few days later I got the itch to wander—Latin verbs always did that to me—and by the time I found my way home again the deed was done; Elizabeth and Quennel were married. You could have knocked me down with a feather—as Elizabeth never made much secret of her low opinion of m'brother. Now, you tell me—was it blackmail or not?''

Patrick chewed on the question for a moment, then answered, "It's all in how you look at it, I imagine. The squire may have felt Quennel was doing him a great favor. After all, the marriage certainly prevented a scandal, although it must have been dreadful for poor Elizabeth. First she lost her beloved William, and then she was forced into marriage with someone she particularly disliked.''

"The squire died alone and quite penniless not six months after the marriage—and he had been comfortably plump in the pocket all his life," Quentin informed the Earl softly. "Quennel saved the squire all right, and then took the man's daughter and fortune for himself. Yes, I call it blackmail.''

"Damme!" Patrick swore savagely, slamming his fist into his palm. "I wish Quennel were still alive so I could take my whip to him. Poor Elizabeth, she must have welcomed death." Then, looking carefully at Quentin, he asked, "Why have you and Willie kept all this from Victoria? I can understand not telling her when she was still a girl, but don't you think it's time she knew? It's not as if you're preserving some fond memory of her father for her, you know. As a matter of fact, I think the knowledge would go a long way toward easing her mind about her less-than-daughterly feelings for the man.''

Quentin took another bracing drink from his glass. ''Willie was only following Elizabeth's instructions,'' he explained, looking into his glass as if for answers. ''I guess poor Elizabeth felt the child would have it bad enough once her mama was dead, without knowing that the man she was living with was no relation to her. Besides, knowing Victoria a bit now m'self, I'd say it wouldn't have taken much for her to confront Quennel with her knowledge and then strike out on her own, as if a young female with no money could make her way alone in this wicked city.''

''But she has you now, Quentin,'' Patrick put in gently. ''You may be no blood relation to her, but you are soon to wed Miss Flint, and it's clear Victoria considers the both of you as family. No, I can't agree with Elizabeth's logic anymore. You have to tell her.''

Quentin drained his glass in one swallow. ''I'll think on it, son,'' he promised quietly. ''I do love the lass, you know. She's a good girl; bright as a penny and has a kind heart. Besides, maybe then she'll give up this silly search for Quennel's murderer. As I said, I think she could be putting herself in real danger.''

Patrick poured the older man another liberal portion of wine. ''Tell me about it, Quentin. I think it's time I hear it all.''

Quinton started off slowly, telling Sherbourne how Victoria had thought the Professor had left her penniless until she had found the first small stack of currency tucked between the pages of one of his daily journals. This one discovery had been followed by others, the bills seemingly placed randomly in various books throughout the library.

"She wasn't looking for money, you understand," he put in to clarify the reason for the search. "She was looking for names that fit the initials P.S."

"Ah, yes," Patrick said. "The notorious snuffbox you told me about. Go on."

"Yes, well, while Victoria was looking for suspects, I started smelling something fishy about this money that kept turning up all over the place. I'm no Methodist, you understand, and I've seen a lot more of life than my dear, innocent niece. I started coming downstairs after she was abed and doing some snooping of my own. It wasn't long before this whole business started to reek to high heaven."

"You found the Professor's hiding place and read his ledger," Sherbourne assumed correctly.

"You didn't look at it, so you don't know that there's nothing there to read. It's just page after page of initials and numbers, sort of like a code," Quentin told him, "but it didn't take me long to figure it out. The initials stand for names and the numbers are the amounts of money he had gotten from each of his victims. Some of them must have been paying Quennel for years. My brother may have told everyone that he was writing a history of the English upper classes, but what he was really doing was digging up any dirt he could find on those poor unsuspecting souls and then taking money *not* to write about them. He hid the money he gouged out of each of them in places that mentioned their names— a sort of filing system, I suppose. Lord, it pains me to think we were related."

Sherbourne stood up and began a slow circuit of the room. "It's beginning to become clear to me now," he said thoughtfully. "My few meetings with Quennel were spent as interviews, with him questioning me about my family history for his manuscript. I was flattered, of course, but when I told him I had already done extensive work on a history myself and didn't see the need to continue our talks, he became quite agitated, telling me that none but a man as dedicated as he could ever possibly prepare the true, definitive history. So it was information for blackmail he was really after, was it?''

Patrick laughed at the thought. ''Let me tell you, friend, your brother would have caught cold there, as my family has always made it a point to be outrageous—and proud of it. We'd probably pay him to *print* what he learned! Oh, well. As for the Professor and myself, we parted in anger, to tell the truth, which is why I cannot understand his reasoning in leaving me his library and manuscripts.''

''Quennel was bloody vain, that's why,'' Quentin said shortly. ''He knew full well that Victoria would sell his books and abandon the project. By turning the stuff over to you, he wanted you to feel obligated to finish it for him so that he could live forever as a great historian. He was devilishly smart, you know. Papa wanted him to go into the church. Wouldn't that have been a rare treat!''

Sherbourne smiled his appreciation of the joke. ''But he was taking quite a chance, if you're right. How was he to know that I wouldn't merely publish his existing research—and heaven knows there are reams of it stacked on these shelves—with my own name on it?''

''He knew you are an honorable man, Patrick, that's how,'' Quinton informed him kindly. ''A successful criminal has to be an extremely good judge of people.''

''Does he now?'' Sherbourne countered dryly. ''Then Quennel certainly missed the mark if he thought Pierre Standish would just bow down to a demand for blackmail. Why, Pierre would kill him where he stood. *Oh my God, it couldn't be!*"

"You're right there, son, it couldn't be," Quentin hastened to tell the Earl, whose face now wore an eloquent expression of pain. "At least I couldn't find any mention of Mr. Standish—or yourself, of course—in the books and journals that held the money, although there's quite a few P.S.'s listed in the ledger. Whatever was in that box Quennel left to him—oh yes, Victoria told me about that—m'brother never made a penny-piece from it."

"Maybe he never had the chance," Patrick ventured against his will. "I don't like this, I don't like it at all. If there's a blackmailed murderer out there somewhere, Victoria's ridiculous investigation may force him into silencing her before he and his secret are uncovered. Quentin, give me the names of the other victims."

Searching among the small stacks of papers scattered over the desktop, Quentin unearthed a small sheet written in Victoria's delicate feminine handwriting and handed it to the Earl. "I have all those with the proper initials right here. Victoria has been going through the journals and writing down any names she could find that have the proper initials. We may have been poking at it from different ends, Puddin' and myself, but we came up with the same names. There's yours, right at the top of the list. You can see she's drawn a line through it. Guess you're off the hook as it were, right?"

Sherbourne studied the list in silence for a few moments. "Three of these gentlemen are dead, Quentin, poor fellows," he said presently. "Victoria has already crossed them off, as well as Peter Smithdon, who's off serving with Wellesley. That leaves Pierre, Philip Spalding, and Sir Perkin Seldon, the same two names Pierre—never mind. Well, let me tell you, Quentin, I don't like it. Burn it, there has to be someone else; some-body you've both overlooked.''

"Why?"

"Why? Can you ask? Because neither Spalding nor Seldon are the sort to murder anybody, that's why!" Wickford gritted, angrily flinging Victoria's list onto the desk. "Spalding is a mincing fop who would swoon at the sight of blood, and Sir Perkin doesn't have the wit."

Quentin lowered his gaze for a moment, considering the thing, then ventured weakly, "Maybe one of them visited Quennel earlier that evening and after he left, a burglar crept in and conked the old bastard on the noggin? That would be a pretty turn of events, wouldn't it?"

Picking up the Professor's ledger of ill-gotten receipts and leafing through the many pages, noting dates that went back almost twenty years, Patrick replied bitterly, "Whoever it was, the fellow deserves a medal. But you're right, Quentin. Victoria has to be stopped. This could get ugly before it's done."

"Then you think it might be Standish? I know he's a particular friend of yours, but you have to admit, he's a bit of an odd, secret person."

"Pierre does have some secret in his past, something that happened to him when he returned home after serv-ing with me in the Peninsula, but although he hasn't felt inclined to confide in me, I can't believe it's so terrible that he'd murder to keep it hidden," Patrick said as if to himself, already heading for the hallway. "I believe I'll go have another talk with him. He'll probably make an utter fool of me for my pains, but Victoria has to be protected at all costs. And tell her what you told me. She won't hate you for it, I promise you, and the infor-mation might just serve to make her abandon her silly scheme before she really and truly lands herself in the briars.''

Quentin sat back in his seat after the Earl's departure, a small, satisfied smile lighting his face just as Wilhelmina entered the room, a full dish of sweetmeats held in her hand as a peace offering. ''My, my. So the wind blows in that quarter, does it?'' he mused aloud, gaining himself a confused glance from the love of his life. ''It's just as I thought. Lord bless the boy. We'll have the Earl of Wickford legshackled to Victoria before he knows what hit him, Willie, and you have my word on it!''

''Of course we will,'' Wilhelmina answered flatly. ''Was there ever any doubt? He may be an earl, but he's a good-hearted lad for all that.''

Quentin rose from his chair and went around the desk to relieve the housekeeper of her sweet burden, tossing three of the sugary confections into his mouth for courage before pressing Wilhelmina into a nearby chair and saying seriously, ''The boy wants us to tell Victoria about William Forester, my love. He says it's for the best.''

''It's best to tell the child she was nearly born on the wrong side of the blanket?'' Wilhelmina asked, cocking her head to one side. ''Elizabeth always said we shouldn't take the chance, even though she was longin' to tell the child about her real father. I don't know, Quentin. But to say she's really a bas—, well, you know. Oh dear me, are you sure?''

''The Earl seems to think it's the lesser of two evils, I guess,'' he answered consideringly. ''Hasn't kept him from tumbling into love with Puddin', has it? Besides, he says it will make Victoria happy. Come on, love, what do you say?''

Wilhelmina pulled the candy dish toward her and selected one of the confections for herself. "I'll think on it, Quentin," she promised, chewing thoughtfully. "I'll just have to think on it."

CHAPTER SIXTEEN

"HEYDAY, MY BOY, I thought it was you," Quentin called out heartily, rising from his comfortable seat in the Quinton drawing room to go into the hallway to greet Patrick and his companion, an exquisitely dressed young man who—rather like some ancient Greek whom Quentin remembered hearing about somewhere—had arrived bearing gifts. "I took care of that little business you suggested during our talk yesterday," he added under his breath as he put his arm through the Earl's and drew him into the room. "Puddin' was pleased no end to hear about her real, er, you know, just like you said, but she's standing fast on continuing the search. Can't figure women, can you?"

"I was afraid of that, my friend," Sherbourne whispered back. "Which makes me glad I planned this evening. You remember our plan, don't you? Good. Perceive our first suspect behind you now." More loudly, he said, "Good evening to you too, my friend," before reaching over to literally push his reluctant companion—who had been hovering in the hallway as if contemplating a last-minute escape—into the room ahead of him. "Please allow me to introduce you to—"

"You'd be Philip Spalding, wouldn't you?" Quentin interrupted, coming forward to grasp Spalding's hand in his fierce grip. "The good Earl sent round a note earlier telling us *you* were the one coming along tonight."

"Quentin," Patrick warned softly. For a conspirator, the Earl thought, friend Quinton was sadly lacking in subtlety.

"Huh?" Quinton asked before realizing he had nearly said too much. "Well, never mind that. Come in, come right in, the both of you, and sit down. The ladies are still primping. Been in a rare dither all day, to say it plainly, with everything at sixes and sevens so that a man feels quite abandoned. What ho? Are those sweetmeats you've got tucked under your arm, friend?" he asked Philip, who was still staring at Quentin, a rather bemused expression on his handsome face.

"Yes, er, yes indeed, sir," Spalding admitted dazedly, finally finding his tongue. "They're for the ladies, you understand," he added swiftly, while taking a firm grip on the box as Quentin looked about to snatch it away.

"Oh, don't be impolite, Philip, old man," Patrick scolded mildly, already subsiding into what appeared to have become his favorite chair in the Quinton household. "Besides, I'll wager Mr. Quinton here would gladly trade you some of that lovely port I see standing over there on that side table, if only you were to let him have a small sampling of the delicious contents of that pretty little box. Wouldn't you, Quentin?" he asked, winking at the older man.

"I would at that, my boy," Quinton answered promptly, already moving toward the drinks table. "The gels will be a while yet, if Willie hasn't put an end to the fuss I heard going on up there as I passed by Victoria's door. Here you go, my boy," he said, handing a generously filled glass to Patrick. "As soft a port as you'll find, too, or at least it should be, considering what it put me back to get it."

"Indeed? Today's prices are intolerable, aren't they,

what with the war and all," Philip said politely, accepting an equally full glass while trying mightily to hide the fact that he thought Mr. Quentin Quinton to be just the least bit common, for, after all, he was a guest in the man's house.

"That's quite a coat you've got on, fella," Quentin remarked jovially, still standing in front of Spalding, his body so close that the younger man involuntarily took a slight step backward. "How many men does it take to get you into it, anyway? I once heard of a fella who used two, one for each sleeve, if I remember it rightly."

"I—why, I—" Philip began falteringly, looking toward Patrick, who returned his look blandly.

"Sit down, man, sit down!" Quentin then motioned, obviously not really interested in the answer to his question. Once Philip has hastened to obey—perching himself gingerly on one small corner of the settee—Quentin also sat, raising his glass to Philip and Patrick before downing its contents as if it were water and leaning forward to say, "So you're Philip Spalding. As I said, I've heard about you," Lowering his voce slightly, he leaned forward and asked confidentially, "Is it true, then? Don't worry that I won't keep it mum. We're all friends here. Tell me true. Do you really bathe in ass's milk?"

"*Patrick*—" Philip sputtered, this time looking in his companion's direction with desperation evident in every perfectly sculpted feature on his handsome face.

Lifting his glass in a sort of salute, Patrick responded interestedly, "Yes, Philip, pray do tell us. You simply cannot know how long I have agonized over the answer to that particular question. Ah, but here are the ladies," he said, rising languidly to his feet. "It appears, Quentin, that we shall have to suspend this delicate discussion until another time."

Quentin also rose, turning toward the open doorway in anticipation of seeing his niece and her young *dame de compagnie* fitted out in their new finery, and his expansive chest swelled proudly at the sight that met his eyes as Victoria and Emma walked into the room.

"Did you ever see two such beauties?" he demanded rhetorically, already advancing toward Victoria, his pudgy hands outstretched in greeting. "I tell you, my fine fellows, you'll have to watch yourselves if you don't want some other enterprising young bucks stealing a march on you. Surrounded by beaux, that's what they'll be, once this night is over."

"Uncle Quentin, do control yourself," Victoria whispered fiercely, coloring hotly as she took his hands in hers and squeezed them in warning.

"Nonsense," Sherbourne admonished in his smooth voice, startling Victoria into giving a slight jump, for she had not noticed him coming to stand beside her, being fully occupied with trying to halt her uncle's embarrassing discourse. "Really, Miss Quinton, you must learn how to handle compliments with more grace. It isn't nice to contradict someone who is praising you."

Turning to look at the Earl for the first time—while maintaining her stern expression only through a commendable act of will, for the Earl of Wickford in evening dress was a sight to soften the strongest resolve—Victoria returned repressively, "I thank you for that information, sir, and please forgive my ignorance. You see, I have had such limited experience in dealing with flattery."

"Ah, that's more like it," Patrick exclaimed, inclining his head in her direction. "After all, what is left to a gentleman after a leading statement like that than to protest vehemently, and then go on to wax poetic over your shell-like ears, glorious hair, and alabaster skin, all of which pale beneath the sunshiny brightness of your smile?''

''I'm not smiling,'' Victoria pointed out unnecessarily, lifting her chin defiantly.

Sherbourne merely shrugged. ''Forgive my lapse, my dear Miss Quinton, which I must tell you, I feel to be totally excusable, considering the fact that your ravishing appearance tonight has so set my treacherous heart to fluttering that I scarce know what to say.''

Victoria looked at Patrick assessingly, her gaze scanning him from top to toe before going back to his face. She was in looks tonight; she knew that because her mirror did not lie, and her newfound sense of herself as a female emboldened her to respond evenly, ''Better, Wickford, better. In fact, I am encouraged to believe that there's hope for you yet.''

Patrick stared back at her, nonplussed for just a moment, before throwing back his head and roaring with appreciation. The awkward miss was fast being replaced by a woman of the world, and he found himself looking forward to the remainder of the evening with every anticipation of being highly entertained.

Suddenly shocked by her display of forwardness, Victoria dropped her gaze to her satin-clad feet, secretly wondering if the new, snug-fitting slippers had somehow cut off the circulation to her head, thereby causing her to lose her customary common sense. But no, she countered mentally, that wasn't it. What had her so lighthearted, so utterly in alt, was the guilt-banishing news she had received the night before—the intelligence that the Professor was *not* her sire.

Indeed, after shedding a few heartfelt tears over the happiness denied her real parents, she had been floating through the hours, feeling almost reborn. She would have to take a firm hold on herself before she disgraced her beloved uncle by allowing her suddenly carefree heart to goad her into breaking into song!

Sensing her embarrassment, and not wishing to have her refining overlong on her rather forward comment, the Earl quickly sought out a diversion. Looking over toward Philip Spalding, who was still staring into Mrs. Hamilton's china-blue eyes with a look that could only be called adoring, Patrick leaned down to whisper to Victoria, "Observe our friend Spalding, Miss Quinton."

Victoria obliged, taking in the man's physical perfection only superficially for, to her, there was no handsomer man in England than the one now standing so close by her side. "He seems much taken with Emma" was all she said, finding vindication in the pressure she had been applying to Emma all day as her companion had tried every ploy in order to find a way not to wear the new finery Quentin had purchased for her for the evening. "One can only hope that he finds her company unexceptionable, for Emma has been most apprehensive about overstepping what she calls her place."

"Put your fears for Mrs. Hamilton to rest, Miss Quinton," Patrick offered bracingly. "If I am any judge, I do believe the gentleman to be utterly in thralldom. It's a sight to warm one's heart, although I do admit to a slight desire to go over there and close his mouth for him, as I do believe he is about to drool all over that pretty waistcoat he's wearing."

Victoria's head turned sharply in Emma's direction. She had forgotten about Philip Spalding, *suspect,* the moment Patrick had approached her, which was unforgivable, as the mission she had set herself for the evening—since learning the man was to be one of their party—involved discovering anything to the point that she could about the man. Frowning slightly as she took in the rapturous look on Emma's face, she said impetuously, "I hadn't planned on this."

Cocking one expressive eyebrow, Sherbourne quipped, "No! Don't tell me *you've* decided to hang out your cap for friend Philip? Dull sport, if you ask me."

"Can't you think of anything other than…than…" Words failed her and she left the sentence dangling as she spread her hands in disgust.

"Other than what, Miss Quinton?" Patrick pursued, not adverse to teasing her a little bit. "Romance? The sweet thrill of the chase? The anticipation of a small dalliance in some secluded garden? Or are my thoughts too ordinary, too tame? Perhaps you, who have enjoyed a lifetime of literary pursuit, are put more in mind of Casanova, or our friend Byron's scribblings—even some of the sentiments expressed by other, yet more worldly poets? Pray, enlighten me, as I wait with bated breath."

"Emma!" Victoria fairly exploded, rushing over to her companion (and away from Lord Wickford), for her new-found sophistication did not extend to listening to any more of Patrick's sallies. "As you have the advantage of me, do you think you could *formally* introduce me to Mr. Spalding?"

Emma, who had been drifting in a dream ever since first setting eyes on the glorious creature who, unbelievably, was returning her gaze with a look of near adoration, literally had to shake herself back to reality to effect the introductions, presenting Victoria as the charge she had been engaged to chaperone.

"Chaperone?" Philip chided solemnly, lifting Emma's hand to his lips. "What utter nonsense. Why, you can be but little removed from the schoolroom your-self.''

"Oh, Mr. Spalding," Emma gushed, schoolgirllike, "surely you are funning me. I'm no such thing. Why, I'm already married...and...and a widow."

"No!" Philip protested vehemently, his rather high, thin voice (the sole blemish that marred his physical perfection, if one was willing to discount his rather shallow mental capacity) quavering with emotion. "I will not hear of it! That you, dearest lady, should have lived in this same world, trod the same earth, breathed the same sweet air, without my knowledge of your existence—why, it defies the imagination! My entire life until this moment is at once a sham, a joke, a hollow wasteland. Only tonight do I begin to live!"

"Oh, Mr. Spalding!" Emma breathed in ecstasy.

"Oh, Mr. Spalding!" Victoria scolded in shock.

"Oh, Mr. Spalding!" Quentin cheered in appreciation.

"Oh, good grief!" Patrick groaned in disgust, immediately earning for himself threatening black looks from the other three observers who, it seemed, agreed with everyone else's sentiments but his.

"You dare to doubt me?" Philip challenged rather shrilly, dropping Emma's hand and turning to confront his detractor. "I tell you, Patrick," he said in awful tones, "much as I responded with raillery when first presented with your plans for this evening, much as I sought excuses to rid myself of the necessity of lending myself to escorting two unknown females to the theatre, I could now go down on my knees to you in thanks."

"No, you couldn't," Patrick pointed out cheerfully. "Your breeches are too tight."

Drawing himself up to his full height, Philip Spalding

reached a hand toward his left pocket, forgetting that he had left his gloves in the hallway, for he had every intention of slapping the Earl of Wickford firmly across his cheek. Dropping his hand back down to his side, he demanded haughtily, "Name your seconds, sir! For now you have gone too far!"

"Willie! Willie!" Quentin bellowed in high good humor, running to the doorway to call the housekeeper before racing back to where Patrick and Philip stood, Sherbourne engagingly attractive in his amusement, Spalding magnficent in his fury. "Willie, you have to see this! They're going to fight a duel over Emma. What a rare treat! Come quick!"

Victoria grabbed onto her uncle's arm, as the agitated man seemed about to explode, and fairly shoved him behind her as she stepped between the two combatants—one now nearly doubled up with laughter, the other now standing quite rigid in his outraged dignity—and faced the Earl.

"Apologize, sir," she ordered, her stern expression not quite hiding her unspoken appreciation of the absolute silliness of the situation. "Poor Emma is nearly distracted with fear. Besides, Willie will be in here at any moment, probably waving a poker in her hand, daring anyone to be so foolish as to even *think* of spilling blood on her carpet."

Wilhelmina did arrive, just as Victoria had predicted, although she arrived brandishing not a poker but a heavy black iron pot, and Patrick, who knew that Philip Spalding's only hope of besting him in a duel lay in the obscure chance that they exchanged calling cards at twenty paces, obligingly offered his apologies all round.

"I accept your apology," Philip said punctiliously, bowing with courtly grace before going over to tuck

Emma's hand protectively through the crook of his elbow. "After all, I cannot forget that it is only because of you that I have been blessed with meeting this wonderful woman."

"Oh, Mr. Spalding," Emma gushed on a sigh.

"Oh, Mr. Spalding," Victoria trilled in warning.

"Oh, Mr. Spalding," Quentin breathed in anticipation.

"Oh no, you don't!" Patrick declared loudly, hastily draping Victoria's evening cloak about her shoulders and giving her a gentle nudge toward the doorway. "I don't believe I can allow this conversation to go any further. Spalding, old fellow, if you can stop ogling that poor lady long enough to help her with her cloak, I do believe we should be departing for the theatre. Quinton, your servant," he ended, already on his way out of the room, Victoria at his side, one hand to her mouth as she hid her involuntary grin of appreciation.

CHAPTER SEVENTEEN

"WHAT A WONDERFULLY comic expression on that actor's face, Miss Quinton," Patrick whispered into Victoria's ear. "But, of course, *The Critic* is one of Sheridan's best, you must agree, giving the actor much to work with. Ah, look now how he's waggling his eyebrows in ludicrous dismay, just so," he ended, aping the actor's facial acrobatics perfectly.

Victoria's eyebrows lowered menacingly as she turned her head slowly to stare daggers at her companion, who stopped waggling his eyebrows in order to grin at her irrepressibly. "Oh, do be quiet," she gritted tersely, hating the man for knowing that her vision of the characters on stage was limited to the coloring of their various costumes; she could barely see their faces, let alone their expressions.

"Then you aren't enjoying the play?" he pushed, feigning innocence.

"It's nice."

"Nice?" Sherbourne repeated. "You admit to this being your first visit to a theatre and after viewing the farce and a full act of Sheridan's play, the best you can do is to say it is nice? Why, my dear Miss Quinton, how you do run on."

Her full lips compressed into a tightly curved bow, Victoria said crushingly, "Lord Wickford...go...to... perdition."

"Isn't this a lovely evening?" Philip Spalding said blithely, leaning front a little to add his bit to the conversation. "I mean, we did have a bit of a pother earlier, that slight contretemps that I am sure we have all quite forgotten; but now, why I do believe we are all as merry as grigs. Aren't we, Em—, er, Mrs. Hamilton?"

"Right you are, Philip," Patrick agreed with a smile. Then, leaning closer to Victoria, he said confidingly, "Dead as a house, friend Philip is, for all his grand appearance."

Lifting her program to cover the fact that she wanted nothing more than to go off into gales of laughter, Victoria turned her attention back to the stage, concentrating on remembering Wilhelmina's warning about squinting in public.

"Please, Miss Quinton," Patrick pursued in all seriousness, once Spalding had removed his face from between them and gone back to staring at Emma like a puppy at his first sign of a meaty bone, "I know you are dying to slip on your spectacles so that you might see what you're looking at. The lights are dim, and I promise not to stand up and whistle everyone's attention to this box."

"I am not quite such a zany, sir," she told him severely, refusing to turn her attention away from the stage. "I would have to be completely blind not to have noticed the stir Emma and I caused arriving in company with you and Mr. Spalding—and stone deaf not to hear the questions and speculations concerning our identities that went winging rapidly through the air while you and Mr. Spalding were disposing of our cloaks. It might interest you to know that we were first thought to be lightskirts, except for the fact that I am not quite pretty enough to fit that role."

Patrick's eyes closed for a moment as he digested what she had said. So that was what had put her in such a strange mood, and after she had seemed so happy earlier. Damn! he silently swore, mentally kicking himself. He should have known that his appearance here with Victoria would cause a stir, especially with the handsome Spalding and the too-young, too-pretty Emma Hamilton acting as chaperone, but the anger her words provoked in him on Victoria's behalf seemed out of proportion to the insult, which was really no more than could have been expected from the gossip-mad *ton*.

"Would you like to retire?" he asked solicitously, already fairly certain of her answer. Miss Quinton, he had learned, was no simpering miss—it would be totally out of character for her to turn craven at the first hurdle.

Victoria turned to look at him, surprising him mightily by giving him a quick glimpse of her seldom-seen dimple as she smiled. "Actually, what I would like to do appalls even me, who has had years of solitude in which to develop a rather fertile imagination."

"You want to put out your tongue at the lot of them?" he asked, grinning a bit himself.

Looking at him askance, Victoria scolded, feeling carefree and happy once again. "And you call yourself a rakehell? For shame!"

"I never call myself a rakehell—I've never found the need," Sherbourne corrected scrupulously. "Now tell me, how would you revenge yourself on these unimportant people if you had the opportunity? I admit to being fascinated."

All at once Victoria was shaken with an almost overpowering urge to take the Earl's lean face between her hands and plant a smacking kiss squarely on his mouth, as all around her gentlemen cheered and ladies swooned.

"I, er, I..." she stammered, realizing she could not voice such outrageous thoughts aloud—most especially to Patrick! "I believe I should like to pour lemonade all over everyone sitting below us in the pit," she substituted swiftly, knowing it to be a paltry revenge indeed.

"I say," Philip Spalding ventured, leaning forward once again, "I hate to interrupt you, but the curtain has come down for intermission. Lemonade, anyone?"

Victoria bit down hard on her bottom lip and immediately took refuge once again behind her program.

"What a splendid good fellow you are, Philip," Patrick said in answer, trying hard not to look at Victoria. "Why don't you and Mrs. Hamilton run along ahead and secure us some before the crush becomes too thick, and we'll join you in a few minutes. Miss Quinton," he added, giving Victoria a quick wink, "you did say you desired lemonade, didn't you?"

"I did," Victoria, her gaze directed toward the empty stage, answered straight-faced, although her amber eyes were twinkling.

Patrick smiled knowingly. Covertly reaching out a hand and placing it warningly on her bare forearm, he said coolly, "Yes. Miss Quinton does indeed desire some lemonade, Spalding, just as you thought. Kindly procure her five dozen glasses, if you please."

"Five dozen gla— *What?*" Spalding gasped.

"You're too kind," Victoria gushed, turning toward Spalding and batting her eyelashes in imitation of an exotic-looking creature she had seen draped on some young buck's arm as they had entered the theatre.

Philip Spalding had a reputation for being kind, considerate, and always willing to put himself out for a lady, but this time he was having second thoughts. "I—I'll, um, I'll see what I can do. Sherbourne," he said in bewilderment before nodding in the Earl's direction and holding out a hand to Emma—who declined to leave her charge. Then he fairly fled from the box just before Patrick and Victoria, feeling very much in tune with each other, collapsed against each other in glee.

CHAPTER EIGHTEEN

THERE DID EXIST in London a few dedicated souls whose primary reason for being in attendance at the theatre that night was to view the goings-on taking place on the stage, but, for the majority, it was those periods of intermission that drew them, dressed in their silks and satins and glittering jewels.

For it was during those precious moments spent in the crowded hallways and foyers behind the boxes where those of the *ton* sat that people knew they would view the real drama of the evening. It was here that they all came, to see and be seen, to be brought up-to-date on the latest scandals, and to indulge in minor intrigues of their own.

During this, the first long intermission of the evening, an impeccably dressed Pierre Standish wended his way easily through the crush of people standing in the wide hallway behind the boxes to the place where Sir Perkin Seldon stood exchanging pleasantries with a minor member of Parliament, the chubby man's usual endearingly vacant grin demonstrating his willingness to agree with anything the ambitious man was saying as Sir Perkin unabashedly used his fingers to eat from the small plate of delicacies balanced in the other man's hand.

"Ah, Sir Perkin, here you are," Pierre drawled urbanely as he came up behind the verbose member of Parliament. "Stuck with yet another prosy bore, I see.

You really must attempt to exhibit more discretion, my dear fellow. It is after all, only a small plate.''

"How dare you! Just who do you think you are to—'' the "prosy bore" objected hotly at once, only to cut short his tirade on a gasp as he turned his head and saw the man he believed he had been about to slice into ribbons with his eloquence; he ended by mumbling something incoherent into his highly starched cravat.

Raising one dark brow the merest fraction, Pierre intoned icily, "My dear fellow, excuse me, but I have no recollection of expressing any desire to have speech with you. Be a good sport, won't you, and toddle off now.''

The man, his face now a most unbecoming shade of puce, obliged by immediately backing up three paces before turning on his heels and disappearing into the crowd, leaving Pierre to remark cordially to Sir Perkin, "I do believe I like that man, don't you? He's so very obedient; much like a spotted terrier I remember from my bucolic youth. Do you think he could be taught to fetch?''

Sir Perkin brought his bushy brown brows together and scratched at his shiny, balding pate before speaking. "He took his plate with him,'' he lamented briefly. "The ham was quite tasty, too.'' Then, his frown deepening, he asked, "Did—did you want to talk to me?''

"Now what idiot was it that said you were slow?'' Standish returned with a slight smile, moving over to lean one strong shoulder against the stuccoed wall, his arms crossed in front of his chest to demonstrate that he was posing no threat to the small, chubby gentleman, but merely passing the time in idle conversation.

"But—but you never have before,'' Sir Perkin pointed out, a bit relaxed, but still quite obviously confused to have been singled out for such exalted—if not exactly sought after—attention. "Not that I mind, you understand," he pushed on quickly, as Standish tilted his head slightly to one side to stare at him inquisitively. "It ain't as if I go around in your circles, so to speak."

"Ah, my dear Sir Perkin—or perhaps you will allow me to call you Sir Perky, as do your intimates?" At the sight of Sir Perkin's eager expression and madly bobbing head, Pierre continued ambiguously, "Thank you, you sweet man. You are indeed as kind as your reputation would have me believe. I cannot imagine why I have waited so long to seek you out, can you?" Standish sighed audibly. "I must only blush as I admit that I do, alas, have an ulterior motive for approaching you at this time. Please forgive me, dear Sir Perky, for I mean to use you for a little project I have in mind."

Sir Perkin swallowed down hard, nearly choking on the bit of ham he had just removed from his pocket and popped into his mouth. "Forgive *you!*" he exclaimed, flattered as only the terribly naive or happily simple-minded can be.

Standish only blinked once and held his tongue, for it was clear his companion was not finished.

"Mr. Standish, I am your servant! I'll dine out for at least a month on just the story about how you routed old Simpson so famously a moment ago, and it's no won-der—with my pockets to let yet again—that I shall trade on it shamelessly," Sir Perkin added candidly, for it was common knowledge that the genial young man was in low water, and not above stuffing his pockets with tidbits from his hostesses' platters in order to feed his ravenous appetite.

Pierre smiled now in genuine amusement as Sir Perkin enlarged on his statement by giving his generous stom-ach a comforting rub at the thought of the delicious joints of fine beef and heaps of sweet pastries soon to be his. Obviously the intoxicating promise of unlimited food had banished any fear of Standish from Sir Perky's head.

CHAPTER NINETEEN

PHILIP SPALDING, being the dependable, trustworthy gentleman that he was, had already found his way to a refreshment booth, procured two glasses of lemonade—and two others containing a somewhat stronger liquid—and was returning to the box just as Patrick escorted Victoria and Mrs. Hamilton into the wide hallway.

"Isn't he just the most handsome, genteel gentleman you have ever seen?" Emma asked Victoria in a breathless voice, squeezing the younger woman's arm to hold her back as Sherbourne walked off in order to meet Philip halfway and relieve him of one of the glasses.

"The Earl?" Victoria asked, tongue in cheek, as she was still in a very good mood, her playful bantering with Patrick having eased any remaining apprehension about having decided that she could eliminate him as a suspect in the Professor's murder.

Emma's lips thinned a bit as she realized she was being teased. "As to the Earl, my dear, I was not so unattending that I did not notice the rather intimate exchange between the two of you when Mr. Spalding left the box. I would be shirking my duty as your chaperone if I did not point out that such familiar behavior is not acceptable. There, I've said it. Now let's enjoy ourselves, shall we?"

Victoria, unused to doing the unacceptable—and delighted to hear that she had—decided to take this gentle rebuke as a compliment to her easy adaptation to a new, more free lifestyle, and only quipped airily, "Am I to infer then that mooning over each other like two lovesick calves *is* acceptable, my dear, levelheaded chaperone?"

Emma's pretty face flushed becomingly, making her look like a young girl. "Oh dear, is it that obvious? I vow I don't recall when I was ever thrown into such a pelter, even when I first met my dearest, departed Harry. Am I being a complete ninny, Victoria, do you think, or am I not being overly optimistic in believing that Mr. Spalding returns my regard?"

Now, here's a dilemma, Victoria thought, frowning. It's as plain as the diamond in Uncle Quentin's cravat that Mr. Spalding is quite enamored of Emma—and she of him—yet, because of his initials and some scant mention of him in the Professor's private papers, he has to remain a murder suspect. Oh, how she wished she could put a period to her investigation! But now, in addition to her own recently amended but still valid (at least in her mind) reason for going on with it, she had to be sure Emma wasn't in danger of falling in love with a murderer. The last, the absolute *last* thing Victoria wanted was to see her delightful widget of a chaperone hurt, and she knew she couldn't guarantee that such a thing wouldn't happen.

"I think Mr. Philip Spalding tumbled instantly and irrevocably into love with you from the first moment you stepped into the drawing room," Victoria said at last, seeing the nervous tears gathering in Emma's big blue eyes as she awaited an answer to her question.

"Oh, Victoria—"

"I also think that Mr. Philip Spalding cannot be entirely dismissed as a suspect in the Professor's murder, if you will forgive my reminding you that his initials match those engraved on the snuffbox I showed you,'' Victoria hastened to add as Emma looked about to swoon with delight. ''I'm sorry, my dear friend, but I do feel responsible for you, dragging you into my investigation this way.'' As she spoke, Victoria crossed her fingers tightly behind her back and wished most earnestly that Philip Spalding was guilty of no sin more serious than an excess of sensibility.

''*Oh!*'' Emma breathed, startled out of her beatific dream. ''I forgot.'' She looked across the room at Spalding, whose return had been delayed by the approach of two other gentlemen, before turning back to Victoria. Then, straightening her back as if preparing to launch herself into battle, she declared in utmost certainty, ''I have never heard such a ridiculous piece of nonsense in my life! That sweet, wonderful man—why, he wouldn't hurt a fly!''

Lifting one gloved hand to her chin, Victoria surveyed Spalding as best she could as all four gentleman approached, while Emma held her breath. ''I think you may be right,'' Victoria said at last, stepping back a pace as it looked like Emma was about to kiss her. ''Mr. Spalding doesn't seem capable of cold-blooded murder. Now, the man walking next to him, well, I do believe you might not find yourself so willing to champion *him*.''

Emma obligingly looked over at the tall, dark gentleman Victoria had indicated. ''That one? Oh my. *Oh my goodness!* Isn't that Pierre Standish?'' she asked in a quavering voice. ''They say he murdered his valet—or maybe it was his groom. Oh dear, whyever would Mr. Spalding wish to present Mr. Standish to us?''

''I rather doubt, dear Emma, that Mr. Spalding had anything to say about it, judging from the outraged ex-

pression on his face,'' Victoria pointed out as her heartbeat began to drum in her ears. What was Sherbourne
about? she asked herself, wondering when it was that
she had lost control of her own investigation. Drat her
blabbermouth uncle, anyway, and drat Patrick Sherbourne for putting his oar in where it was neither wanted
nor needed! Swallowing down hard on her mingled anger and apprehension, she went on: ''Mr. Standish is a
friend of the Earl's, you see, although I don't believe I
know the fourth gentleman.''

Emma, who had deliberately fastened her gaze on the
floor, looked up quickly before averting her gaze to the
carpet once more. ''Oh, that's only Sir Perky,'' she told
Victoria dismissively. ''I went down to supper with him
once when I was first presented—before I met Harry, of
course. The man gobbled up everything on my plate!
But he's a sweet person, or at least he was then. Why
would he be with Mr. Standish, do you suppose? It
seems so—''

''Why, thank you, Mr. Spalding,'' Victoria said
clearly, warning Emma into silence as she reached out
a hand to remove a glass of lemonade from the tray the
man had proffered with a slight bow. ''Emma, do stop
fretting about that uneven hem and look here—Mr. Spalding has thoughtfully brought us some refreshments.
And some company?'' she ended tentatively, tilting her
head to one side as she looked directly into Standish's
dark eyes and tried her best not to look frightened.

''Ah, the diplomatic Miss Quinton,'' Pierre said, bowing deeply from the waist, ''we meet at last. I have been
out of the city, you understand, and could not resist rushing to the theatre when I returned and found the Earl's
message telling me he would be present here tonight.
Such a dear man, such a good friend,'' he added scru-

pulously, turning to smile at Sherbourne, who was standing in thin-lipped silence. "Isn't that right, my dearest Patrick?"

"I have been trying to reach you since yesterday," the Earl replied shortly, a slight tic working in his cheek.

"Ah, yes," Pierre purred softly, neatly noting Patrick's agitation before turning back to Victoria and continuing suavely, "but I digress. When the dear Earl informed me that you were one of his party, why, I was quite naturally nearly overcome! Please, dear madam, allow me to at last apologize for my rudeness at not introducing myself after the reading of the Professor's will, but I had a pressing appointment and had to rush off."

"Really?" Victoria replied sweetly, only inclining her head slightly in acknowledgment of his bow. "I would have said your rush was more in the nature of a hasty retreat, if I am remembering the occasion correctly. I am so relieved to learn otherwise."

Patrick moved to stand beside Victoria as Pierre reached up to stroke the thin line of his scar with one manicured fingertip. "I believe the word you are searching for, Pierre my friend, is *touché*. Miss Quinton, would you please be so kind as to allow me to present to you and Mrs. Hamilton these two upstanding gentlemen— Mr. Pierre Standish and Sir Perkin Seldon?"

As Patrick identified the second man, Victoria's head turned sharply to look at Pierre, her eyes narrowed in speculation before widening at the look of smug satisfaction evident on his face. "Sir Perky" was really Sir Perkin Seldon—the fourth suspect? But how?... *Oh no! They both know! What did Uncle do—take an advertisement in* The Times? she thought wildly, her hands clenching at her sides momentarily as she silently cursed her prattlebox Uncle Quentin, who had admitted to her only last night that he had been keeping the Earl informed of all their discoveries about the Professor. Now Standish knew as well, and—dreadful beast that he was—the rotter was laughing at her! It is small comfort, she thought, that neither of the gentlemen knows about my true parentage, but it is absolutely the *only* thing that is keeping my feet from carrying me off somewhere private posthaste, where I might scream my vexation to the skies!

"Miss Quinton?" Patrick prodded, looking at her expectantly. "You have already acknowledged Mr. Standish—in a manner of speaking. Surely you don't wish to cut poor Sir Perkin, do you?"

Victoria opened her mouth to speak, then shut it again in order to collect her thoughts. This was what she had wanted—to be presented to Society and meet all four of the suspects she had gleaned from the Professor's papers—so why was she feeling so empty, so unbelievably disappointed?

She hadn't really believed that Patrick Sherbourne had taken a personal interest in her, had she? She couldn't have pinned her spinsterish hopes on his falling madly, passionately in love with her, could she? How could she—normally a most sensible person—have entertained, for even an instant, the ridiculous idea that the Earl had visions of romance in mind when he had issued his invitation to the theatre?

She should have realized that he was only funning with her, helping her as it were, in her "quixotic quest" (she flinched slightly as she recalled the term) to discover the Professor's murderer. And now, just to make matters worse, he had included his crony Pierre Standish in his scheme. Oh Victoria, she rued silently, only a silly spinster at her last prayers could have been so lamentably gullible!

Emma, sensing Victoria's tenseness, although not yet realizing that *all four* men standing in front of her bore the same possibly damning initials, stepped neatly into the breach as a proper chaperone should do, saying, "Sir Perkin, I vow it's been an age. I doubt you remember me at all. Of course, I was Emma Connington then."

Sir Perkin answered Emma absently, his rather small brown eyes intent on the person of Victoria Quinton. "Ain't she the daughter of that Professor fellow who slipped his wind some weeks ago?" he said, as if to himself. "No, couldn't be her. Not in mourning, is she?"

"Don't be vulgar, darling," Pierre breathed softly, "else I shall be forced to drop you."

But it was too late, for Victoria had come out of her brown study in time to hear Sir Perkin's words. "The Professor didn't wish for me to go into mourning, sir, and as an obedient, er, daughter, I have obliged. But tell me, how did you come to know the Professor? I don't believe I recall ever seeing you in Ablemarle Street."

Sir Perkin reached into his pockets with both hands, searching until he unearthed a crust of bread he had placed there earlier after dining at Lady Sefton's, and then popped the comforting morsel into his mouth. "I don't recall," he answered around the lump in his chubby cheek. "Ablemarle Street, you say? No, no, that wasn't it. I met him here and there, I imagine. I say, isn't that the warning bell? Best take our seats if we want to see the next act, right?" he said in a rush, already taking his leave.

"Do stay, dear Sir Perky," Standish commanded softly, halting the man in his tracks.

"Sir Perky's right, Standish," Philip Spalding put in scrupulously, looking about for a table on which to deposit the empty glasses he had thoughtfully gathered from his companions. "It wouldn't be proper to have the ladies miss a portion of their first theatre performance by standing about for a few minutes of idle chatter in the hallway."

"I stand corrected, of course," Pierre said bowing once again. "As usual, my dearest Philip, you are the epitome of polite behavior, while I remain the rudest beast in nature, attempting to steal a few more precious moments of Miss Quinton's delightful company. And yours as well, my dear Mrs. Hamilton. Ladies, your most obedient," he drawled softly before slipping a hand around Sir Perkin's elbow. "Come along, my informative friend, as I do believe you have served your purpose. I suggest we retire to White's, where I imagine they may be prevailed upon to serve us a late supper."

"Do you suppose they have ham?" Sir Perky queried anxiously as he allowed himself to be led off like an obedient puppy, its stubby tail wagging furiously in happy anticipation of a treat for performing as asked. "I'm particularly fond of ham, you know. Goodbye!" he remembered to call over his shoulder as he skipped along behind the long-legged Standish. "Been a pleasure and all that."

"Wasn't that odd?" Philip opined before dismissing the two gentlemen from his mind as he made to escort Emma back to her chair. "Has anyone ever remarked, my dear Mrs. Hamilton, on the absolute perfection of your earlobes?" Victoria could hear him saying as the two lovebirds drifted away.

"Miss Quinton?" Patrick then nudged, holding out his arm so that she might take it.

At last Victoria was free to speak her mind, and she immediately went on the attack. "You planned the whole ridiculous charade that occurred just now, didn't you?" she accused angrily, taking his arm with much more force than was proper. "You and that supercilious Pierre Standish. That's the only reason you offered to escort me here this evening, isn't it? Don't bother to protest your innocence to me, as I shan't believe a word of it," she rushed on as the Earl tried to slide in a word or two in his own defense. "Uncle Quentin told me that he had confided his fears for me in you, but then that poor, sweet, impressionable man couldn't have known that you'd then go haring off—rubbing your hands together in gleeful anticipation, no doubt—to spill the soup to Mr. Standish so that the two of you could concoct some silly schoolboy plot to unmask the murderer. And, please, I beg of you, *don't* go trying to fob me off with some farradiddle about doing it to *protect* me. You're enjoying yourself mightily," she fairly sneered, "and don't dare to deny it."

"One question at a time, if you please. As to your first question, I planned *half* of it," Patrick admitted, easing her tightly grasping fingers slightly away from the material of his jacket sleeve. "Once I knew exactly why Standish and I were suspects, I felt honor-bound to inform him of his position. It was my idea to bring Spalding along tonight, but Pierre has always been rather independent, and he must have decided to round up Sir Perky for you as well.

"By the by," he continued quietly, so that he could not be overheard by the few persons still strolling about the hallway, "even though I wasn't going to bring up the subject tonight, you must know that you have my deepest sympathy, my dear. Your life with Quennel

Quinton must have been nearly intolerable. Indeed, Pierre was quite overcome when I had told him the whole of it—gave me his word then and there to help you in any way he could. Although you probably will refuse to understand it, you should be considering yourself quite honored. Pierre doesn't go out of his way for anyone very often.''

"You know that he thinks he did it, don't you?" Victoria declared, still refusing to move.

"Perhaps you would clarify that a bit, please? Who do you mean by the second 'he'?"

"Mr. Standish thinks Sir Perkin Seldon is the murderer, of course," she spat back at him. "It's as plain as that scar on *his*—Standish's, I mean—face."

"Sir Perky a murderer? That harmless nodcock? Don't be ridiculous.'' So she had caught on to Pierre's cryptic remark about Sir Perky serving "his purpose," had she? Patrick's estimation of Victoria's intelligence, already high, increased by another giant leap.

Victoria sniffed her derision. "Ridiculous is precisely what I would be if I ever believed anything Pierre Standish had to say. The man is totally evil. Why, Emma told me just tonight that he has already murdered his valet.''

"His groom," Sherbourne corrected. "That's old gossip. Besides, the man had the bad judgment to come at Pierre with a knife.''

"With good reason, no doubt.''

"So you've decided on Standish, then?" Patrick pursued thoughtfully, moving to face her in the now-empty hallway. "While I am greatly relieved to hear that you have abandoned your intention to see me swing from the gibbet, I find I must protest. I know the man well, and Pierre Standish is no murderer.''

"And I'm no debutante," Victoria said coldly. "As the farce is now over, I believe I should like you to take me home. After all, there is nothing left for you to do tonight."

"Isn't there? You forget—I haven't yet answered your second question. If I recall correctly, it had something to do with my motive for escorting you here this evening. Perhaps this will serve as your answer," Patrick rasped in a low, determined voice before hauling her roughly into his arms.

Stepping out of Lady Wentworth's box in order to get away from her cloying perfume, George Brummell chanced to look to his left in time to see Patrick Sherbourne and Miss Victoria Quinton locked in a rather torrid embrace in the shadows.

Lifting his quizzing glass to his eye, Beau drawled thoughtfully, "How ex-treme-ly in-ter-est-ing. Per-haps *I* shan't be needed af-ter all," before quietly stepping back the way he had come.

CHAPTER TWENTY

"IF I MIGHT SAY SO, Victoria my dear, you look a trifle cast down," Emma Hamilton commented, looking up from the small embroidery square she was working on as she bore her charge company in the sunlit Quinton library. "Perhaps the headache that intruded on last night's foray to the theatre has not fully abated. I could ask Miss Flint for some camphorated spirits of lavender, if you wish."

Victoria looked up from the Professor's vastly boring daily journal for the year 1810, which she had been studying for the past half hour (without really registering anything she had read), and removed her spectacles. Resting them on the desk, she reached up to massage her throbbing temples. "I'm really quite all right, Emma, thank you. It was so silly, you know, as I am rarely ever ill. I'm only sorry I had to cut short your evening. Mr. Spalding was most disappointed."

Emma's pretty face took on an adorably bemused expression. "He was sweet, wasn't he? I had half hoped that he'd pay a morning call today, but—"

"That would explain why you have deigned to wear one of the new gowns Uncle Quentin purchased," Victoria commented, smiling a bit in spite of her depressed mood. "That is a most becoming style."

Looking down at the flattering pink muslin gown that showed her petite figure to such advantage, Emma sighed soulfully, then said in a sad voice, "Yes, but as the hour grows late, I am realizing the foolishness of my hopes. Mr. Spalding is just the dearest, the sweetest gentleman I have ever met, but he must have realized that he is quite too important in Society to consider showing an interest in a Nobody like me."

Victoria suddenly realized she was feeling even sorrier for her youthful chaperone than she was for herself. After all, at least she herself had not been foolish enough to consider that Patrick's impulsive actions at the theatre had really *meant* anything, had she? She shook her head emphatically and picked up her spectacles, once more anchoring the thin metal arms firmly around her ears. "True love does not regard such mundane things as social prominence as obstacles, Emma," she said kindly, knowing she sounded like one of the birdwitted characters in the marble-backed romances she loved so well. "If Mr. Spalding is genuinely attracted to you, he will find his way to Ablemarle Street—if not today, then very soon."

Emma looked across at Victoria, who had already picked up the journal again and was now looking completely engrossed in what she found there. "You're so very level-headed, Victoria," she breathed in real admiration. "Another young woman would have let her head be turned upon finding herself the recipient of the attentions of anyone as handsome and rich and well placed as the Earl of Wickford—but you have not let it deter you so much as a jot from your original plan of unmasking your dear departed father's murderer."

Victoria bit her bottom lip on the admission that nearly slipped out—an admission that could leave the gentle Emma no choice but to think her an unnatural "daughter." "Please, my dear friend," she pleaded at last, "don't try to make me into some sort of paragon, for I assure you, I am not."

"Of course you are, Victoria," Emma protested hotly. "Why, look at you now! Only last night you had to leave the theatre early because you were ill; yet here you are, hard at work again the very next day. I feel so shallow and flighty, taxing you with my silly problems. How could I be such a thoughtless widget? Please forgive me!"

Slapping the journal down onto the desk with a bit more force than necessary, Victoria rose to her feet and came round to the front of the desk to face her friend. "Emma..." she began slowly, searching for the right words to confide in the other woman her *real* reason for deliberately trying to lose herself in work this morning, which was the *same* reason that she had pleaded a headache at the theatre the previous evening, and the *same* reason that she had spent the remainder of that endless night sleeplessly pacing her chamber.

"I bid you good morning, ladies."

Victoria wheeled sharply to see the Earl of Wickford stepping jauntily into the room, his curly brimmed beaver held in one hand, a highly polished wooden cane tucked under his other arm. He looked so handsome standing there in his impeccably tailored clothing that she suddenly found it difficult to breathe, let alone return his greeting.

"Miss Flint is busy in the foyer industriously attacking the bannister with some vile-smelling compound, so I volunteered to find my own way to the library. Mrs. Hamilton," he continued, turning to bow to Emma, "I discovered a certain lovesick young fellow lurking about outside on the doorstep as I approached, a rather lovely bouquet of flowers clenched in his paw."

"Oh!" Emma exclaimed, her hands going immediately to her perfectly arranged curls.

"Yes, indeed," Patrick drawled in amusement. "It was none other than our friend Mr. Philip Spalding. I put him in the drawing room for you, if that's all right? If you keep the door to the foyer open, I'm sure Miss Flint will be happy to act as chaperone."

Emma had risen halfway out of her chair, her embroidery square slipping to the floor unheeded, when she realized that she could not allow her charge to be alone with the Earl. Looking from Sherbourne to Victoria and then back again, mute appeal in her eyes, she asked anxiously, "Whatever shall I do? This has never happened to me before, you understand, as I have never had a gentleman caller since poor Harry died."

"If you will allow me to suggest a solution, Mrs. Hamilton," Patrick said gently, "I do believe you might recall that the door to this room likewise opens onto the foyer. There's a lot to be said for small houses, is there not?"

"Yes!" Emma returned with unladylike enthusiasm, already heading for the doorway as Patrick slowly advanced across the carpeting, his gaze now firmly locked on Victoria's face. But before she could reach the hallway, Emma halted and turned to face her friend. "Victoria?" she breathed softly.

Standing very rigid and still, her gaze never leaving that of the man now standing a mere three feet away from her, Victoria answered tonelessly, "It's all right, Emma, run along," just as if her heart wasn't threatening to burst out of her breast.

"So?" Patrick asked Victoria in a low, amused voice when the silence which descended after Emma left the room had stretched to nearly a full minute. "I'm waiting. Are you going to deliver that sharp slap to my face that you neglected to inflict last evening in favor of pleading a non-existent headache, or are you contemplating something entirely different? A friendly hello kiss would be nice, don't you think?"

Victoria opened her mouth and then shut it again with a snap before closing her eyes tightly and saying from between clenched teeth, "How can you be so provoking!"

Sherbourne grinned as he reached to gently remove Victoria's spectacles, causing her amber eyes to open wide in shock. "How can you be so adorably easy to provoke?" he countered, stepping past her to lay the spectacles on the desktop before turning around and taking hold of her shoulders so that he could place a short, gentle kiss on her lips.

"Hello, Miss Victoria Quinton," he said huskily, loosening his grip and stepping slightly away from her.

Her amber eyes clouded momentarily, then sparkled angrily as she decided that the horrible man was amusing himself by trifling with her. "You are an out and out libertine!" she spat in some heat, beginning to pace swiftly up and down the length of the library, unable to stand still, yet remembering to keep her voice lowered so as not to have to deal with an infuriated housekeeper as well as an insufferable earl.

"That's me down to the ground all right," Patrick agreed amicably, resting lightly against the edge of the desk and watching interestedly as Victoria concentrated her pacing to a small area in front of him, the hem of her becoming light green sprigged muslin gown kicking out in front of her with each agitated step she took.

"Dead to all sense of shame, that's what you are,"

she went on passionately, waving her arms impotently. "You're not in the least penitent, are you? You're such an incorrigible flirt that you cannot even keep yourself in check when faced with such an unimpressive specimen as myself."

"Now I do believe I must object," Patrick countered suavely, pushing himself away from the desk to step in front of her, successfully putting an end to her tirade. "You may still be a bit scrawny, and maybe even a little fusty in your notions, but I wouldn't go so far as to say you're unimpressive.

"As a matter of fact," he went on doggedly when it looked as if Victoria was about to speak once more, "it would flatter you no end if I were to tell you that I am beginning to think of you as quite beautiful—in your own way—and extremely appealing. I even like the spectacles."

Victoria was going to faint, she was sure of it. Her body was hot and cold at the same time, her limbs were trembling almost uncontrollably, and she seemed to have a cannonball lodged partway between her throat and her stomach. She opened her mouth to speak, to ask one of the several thousand questions she could think of, and croaked weakly, "You really like my spectacles?"

Patrick took another step forward, putting himself so close to her that she could feel his warm breath against her cheek as he leaned over slightly and said, "I positively adore them. I have dreams about them. I envy the fact that they are allowed such intimate contact with your petal-soft ears, your magnificent amber eyes, your perfect little nose."

"My nose is ordinary," she mumbled inanely, staring intently at his wondrously tied cravat. "It's just there to keep my eyes apart." Oh Lord, she thought silently, I sound like the village idiot! Why can't I say anything intelligent? Why can I hear my own heart beating? *Why,* she screamed silently as Sherbourne slowly lowered his head and began moving his mouth along one side of her elegantly long throat, *am I asking myself silly questions?* "Oh Patrick," she breathed, tilting her head ever so slightly so as to give him better access to the tender flesh underlining her jaw.

His lips blazed a white-hot trail along the fine line of her jaw and up over her chin, then began nibbling at the sensitive corners of her mouth until her own lips opened under the gentle assault and she gave herself up totally to his questing mouth, his strong arms, *and* his lean, hard body.

"Missy, I've finished with the bannister, and now I'll be wantin' to get in here and—*Oh Lord above, would you look at that! Quentin! Quentin Quinton, you come in here this minute and look at your niece!*" In an instant, Wilhelmina was gone, hotfooting off on the trail of Victoria's uncle.

At the sound of Wilhelmina Flint's shrill shrieks, Victoria had tried to jump away from Patrick's embrace, but he had held her fast against his broad chest, his strong arms still around her as if in protection. "Be still, my darling," he now admonished softly. "I do believe it would be best if I handle things from here on out."

"Dffft mfffnn mmmff!"

Patrick put a hand behind Victoria's neck and lifted her head slightly away from his chest. "What was that, my love? I'm afraid I wasn't attending. Tell me, does your uncle have any pistols in the house?"

"I *said,*" Victoria gulped, trying to catch her breath, "don't do anything rash. I mean, after all, it's not like Willie is about to go screaming through the *ton* that you've compromised me or anything. Uncle Quentin is a man of the world; he'll understand. You had a momentary lapse, a, er, a sudden brainstorm, and shouldn't be held accountable for your actions. Besides, there's something about me you don't know. There's more than one scandal attached to me. You see, I'm not really the Professor's—''

''You couldn't have said all that,'' Patrick interrupted, smiling down at her before pushing her face back against his jacket front in order to shut off her impromptu confession, believing that, although there was a time and place for everything, this was neither. ''As a matter of fact, you barely had time to *think* it. Now hush, pet, as methinks I hear the gentle footfalls of your uncle treading in this direction.''

''Wickford?'' Quentin Quinton rasped, still panting after his rapid descent of the stairs, Wilhelmina's prodding voice hurrying him as he went. ''Willie's locked Emma and Mr. Spalding in the drawing room and told me to get myself into the library because you're mauling my Puddin'. She don't look mauled to me. The child looks damned comfortable, as a matter of fact. What's going on, my boy?''

''Felicitate me, Quentin,'' Patrick answered calmly, trying not to look like he was struggling to hold on to Victoria, who had begun squirming the moment her uncle had entered the room. ''Your niece has just made me the happiest of men by graciously consenting to become my wife.''

''She has!'' Quentin shouted happily, her cherubic face splitting ear to ear in a wide grin.

''I have?'' Victoria questioned wonderfully—and somewhat breathlessly, having at last freed herself.

''You have,'' Patrick pronounced calmly, sliding his

arm around her waist and pulling her gently against his side.

"I didn't—"

"Yes, you did."

"I did? When?"

"Just now, you silly goose."

"Just now—*Ah*, you mean *just now!*"

"Precisely."

"Oh dear. But—"

All at once Quentin was upon them, lifting the bewildered Victoria into a crushing bear hug before setting her back down, grabbing onto the Earl's right hand and shaking it with considerable energy as he exclaimed happily, "I knew it was coming, you know. Oh yes, I did. Ask Willie, she'll tell you. Fell in love with her mind, didn't you? Bright blue she is, though she doesn't hit you over the head with it. Anybody can have a pretty face, right? My Puddin' here, well, she sort of grows on a body, slow-like."

"Like moss, as Emma hinted? Or perhaps you were thinking of a barnacle?" Victoria put in recklessly, beginning to believe that the Earl was serious—he actually meant to wed her.

Quentin grabbed Victoria's cheeks between his chubby, beringed hands and planted a kiss on her mouth. "See, what did I tell you! Sharp as a tack, that's my Puddin'!"

Sherbourne stood silently by until Quentin seemed to wind himself down, then suggested the man round up Wilhelmina and the unsuspecting couple she was holding prisoner in the drawing room so that they could all drink a toast to the up-coming nuptials, which he intended to have take place just as soon as possible without appearing unseemly.

Once Quinton had gone off to take charge of selecting just the proper vintage for a toast of this magnitude, Patrick turned to Victoria, a tender smile lighting his eyes. "You knew last night, of course, didn't you, my dearest love?"

Victoria gazed up at him unblinkingly.

"That was quite a convincing performance of out-raged womanhood you put on earlier, but I understood that you didn't want to appear too anxious, knowing I had come here this morning with the express purpose of proposing to you. That's why I goaded you so shame-lessly, to give you an opening."

"It was? You did?" Victoria blinked twice, trying to understand.

"Yes, of course I did. After all, you're an intelligent little minx, just like Quentin said. You had to know that I had to have been overcome with passion in order to be so rash as to kiss you in public, where all the world and his wife could see us. I nearly declared my inten-tions then and there, except for your nervous headache. But I'm glad I waited, although I will agree that this is not quite the romantic proposal I had envisioned, what with the entire household surrounding us."

A small crease appeared between Victoria's straight brows as she considered his words. He actually felt pas-sion for her—she who only a few short weeks ago had felt her future lay in the bloodless profession of tending other people's offspring. "Wel-l-ll," she began slowly, considering what she should say. She may not be all that worldly-wise, but she instinctively knew that the last, the very last thing she should ever do would be to admit that she hadn't had the faintest suspicion of his inten-tions.

"Yes, pet?" he prodded, smiling down at her.

"Well, I don't wish to appear smug, Patrick, but I am, after all, a woman—"

"Not yet, my dearest darling," Patrick corrected mischievously, giving her rounded bottom a little squeeze. "That doesn't come until *after* the wedding."

"Oh!" Victoria exclaimed, blushing hotly just as Quentin and Wilhelmina came into the room loaded down with wineglasses and bottles of champagne, Emma and Philip in their wake, looking slightly bemused by it all.

"And never mind searching out my meaning in one of your books," he whispered in her ear before releasing her to accept Wilhelmina's effusive congratulations. "I do believe this is one question I'd prefer to answer myself!"

IT WASN'T UNTIL the impromptu betrothal party had wound down and the happy couple was left alone in the drawing room for the few minutes Emma felt were allowable under the circumstances that Victoria, her cheeks weary from smiling, took Patrick by the hand and led him to the settee. "I have something to tell you, my dearest. Something you should have been told before I allowed you to declare yourself," she began solemnly. "At first I was too overcome, and then I thought Uncle Quentin would take you to one side and inform you— but I can see that it is left to me, after all."

Patrick drew her hands into his and smiled soothingly, an endearingly loverlike expression of concern on his handsome face. "Sits it serious, my love?" he asked, already knowing what she was about to disclose. "Have you another fiancé hidden away somewhere whom I should know about?"

Victoria could feel the first stinging of the tears that

were gathering behind her eyes as she shook her head and blurted out, "I have another *father* hidden away in my past, Patrick. The Professor married my mother knowing she was carrying another man's child!"

"What?" Sherbourne exclaimed, feigning surprise. "But how absolutely wonderful! It's comforting to know that this penchant for blackmailing isn't going to spring up somewhere down the line in our children."

"But—but, I'm a bastard," Victoria stammered. "At least, I think I am, technically. Doesn't that concern you in the slightest?"

"My second cousin Ferdy is rumored to be one of Prinney's covey of misbegotten offspring," the Earl countered, shrugging his shoulders as if to dismiss the subject. "I can't see where it makes a halfpenny of difference if your father was the son of a doc—*whoops!*"

"You knew!" Victoria exploded, pulling away her hands and bolting to her feet to stand looking down at the love of her life in accusation. "I should have known Uncle Quentin couldn't be trusted to keep silent. I vow that man's tongue is hinged at both ends!"

Patrick rose to stand beside her and slipped his arms around her stiff frame, pulling her against him as he soothed, "Quentin means well, my darling. Besides, what does it matter—if we love each other?"

After sniffling inelegantly a time or two, Victoria raised her tear-drenched eyes to the Earl's face. "I do love you," she breathed softly, her bottom lip trembling just a bit.

"And I do love you," Patrick responded intensely, his arms tightening fractionally as he drew her more fully into his embrace. Then, easing the tense moment by employing one of his engaging grins, he added, "Convenient, isn't it, how that works out?"

CHAPTER TWENTY-ONE

THE NEXT WEEK PASSED in a dizzying daze of happiness for Victoria, who had finally come to accept the fact that Patrick Sherbourne, Earl of Wickford, was truly in love with her—no matter who she was—and wanted her to be his Countess. The beautiful ancestral betrothal ring of emeralds and diamonds encircling her finger proved it; the notice in the *Morning Post* proved it; the hustle and bustle of trying to gather her bride clothes in time for the wedding planned for the end of June proved it.

But most of all, Patrick himself proved it. He was endlessly loving, he was almost embarrassingly attentive, he was almost comical in his attempts to pull her behind closed doors in order to embrace her, and, best of all, he had agreed to help her solve the mystery of the Professor's death once and for all.

Although she couldn't quite agree with him and Quentin that she was in danger as long as the murderer might decide that he was still open to blackmail while the Professor's daughter was still alive, she allowed them to believe she did. After all, if Patrick knew her *real* reason for continuing the investigation (the one that had superseded every other reason she might have had previous to learning exactly what the contents of the Professor's ledger meant), he might just lock her in her bedchamber until the culprit was in gaol!

So in love was she that she had even agreed to allow

Pierre Standish a small part in the investigation. It wasn't that she still thought him to be guilty that made her reluctant to have Standish included in their plans, she had explained to Patrick; it was just that his friend made her nervous. He seemed to see everything, know everything—while the air of mystery that surrounded him resembled nothing more than a cold, impregnable fog.

By now Victoria, Patrick, and Quentin had been able to piece together the reasons behind each of the Professor's blackmail threats, using the information listed on the pages in his various journals where the packets of money had been discovered. At times damning, at other times downright silly, the reasons were many and varied, but all had seemed important enough to each victim to have him paying for their suppression in the Professor's "history."

After several informal meetings—peppered with Quentin Quinton's highly imaginative suggestions for ways to snare the murderer—it was Patrick who at last came up with the idea of placing both of the remaining suspects together in the same room and revealing the reasons they had been blackmailed in the first place—thus startling one of them into confessing.

It was to this end that Sherbourne had engineered the small, informal dinner party that was now taking place in the narrow house in Ablemarle Street, with Quentin Quinton cast in the role of host. Victoria and Patrick would have leading roles in the execution of their plan, and Patrick—with Victoria's reluctant agreement—had tracked Pierre down at one of his clubs, brought him up-to-date on just what was going forward, and then gained his promise of assistance in case things "got sticky."

Victoria stood near the doorway, dressed in a becoming ivory gown of finest watered silk; the soft brown ringlets that Wilhelmina had earlier combed so carefully over the curling stick framed her face while she watched the proceedings attentively. Slowly the room filled with guests—and murder suspects.

Patrick, looking even more handsome than usual in his severely tailored midnight-blue evening clothes, his dark blond hair showing an endearing tendency to fall forward onto his forehead, was standing beside Victoria, his hand reassuringly cupped around her elbow.

Sir Perkin Seldon, never tardy when free food was to be had, arrived a full quarter hour early, rushing through his expressions of delight at the engagement he had read about in the *Post* in order to divest the passing Wilhelmina of a heavy silver tray containing a multitude of fancy sandwiches which now, its contents badly depleted, resided on his generous lap as he reclined comfortably in Patrick's favorite chair.

Philip Spalding had been the second to arrive, bearing gifts for everyone as usual, and was already firmly ensconced on the drawing room settee beside a flustered Emma Hamilton, reading to her from an ode he had written, "To the Dimple in Her Rounded Chin."

The suspects now both in residence, they were awaiting only the arrival of their co-conspirator, Pierre Standish, who had told Patrick he would be happy to attend the party because "I have always been partial to the farce."

"Mr. Standish is late," Victoria whispered in Patrick's ear, waggling her fingers politely in Sir Perkin's direction as that man tried to get her attention. "You don't suppose he's changed his mind and decided not to—Oh, drat it anyway, what does that silly man want? Patrick, dear heart, please go see what's bothering Sir Perkin."

Looking over to where Sir Perkin sat gesturing very pointedly to the empty side of the silver tray, Patrick hazarded a guess at the problem. "I believe the slivered ham sandwiches Willie labored over were a tremendous hit with the man, though both the tongue and cucumber concoctions missed the mark. Excuse me a moment, my love, while I go search out your housekeeper before Sir Perky fades away to a mere shadow of himself."

"Do that, darling," Pierre Standish drawled urbanely, causing Victoria to utter an audible gasp, as she had not realized that he had at last arrived. "It will give me a moment to attempt to persuade Miss Quinton of the folly of her actions, agreeing to wed one such as you when everyone knows I am by far the better man."

"That you are, Pierre, you sly dog." Sherbourne grinned, clasping Standish's hand in greeting. "Why else do you think I snapped her up so quickly, before you could steal a march on me? I hope you're ready to play your part in our little melodrama?"

"Can you ask?" he answered, raising one expressive eyebrow. "I might even be inspired enough to create a small plot twist of my own, just to ensure that everyone has a lively evening."

"How good of you to come, Mr. Standish," Victoria said, wishing yet again she could feel more at her ease in the man's presence. "My uncle has gone off to seek out another bottle of sherry, but he should be back shortly. Ah, here he is now. Uncle Quentin," she called out quietly, stopping Quinton as he was just about to walk past them, a dusty bottle in one hand. "Our final guest has arrived. Please come over here and allow me to introduce you."

"My dear Mr. Quinton," Pierre said, bowing slightly

in the older man's direction, "it's good to see you again."

"Good to see you too," Quentin responded, transferring the bottle to his left hand before wiping his right hand on his coat and extending it politely. "Er, we've met?"

Pierre's dark face took on a hurt expression. "How soon they forget," he bemoaned to Patrick, who was looking confused and a bit wary. "Let me see if I can jog your memory, dear sir. Two months ago, at Ramsgate? A rather well-endowed barmaid named Rosie, I believe? I had docked my yacht there and retired to a nearby inn for a meal. Does it come back to you now, my dear fellow?"

Quinton's lively blue eyes widened in shock. Looking about himself swiftly for any sign of Wilhelmina, he leaned close to Pierre and whispered urgently, "Keep your voice down, sir, I implore you. I had been at sea quite a long time, you understand, and needed a bit of comfort. Please, I'm soon to become a happily married man!"

"Your distress affects me deeply," Pierre replied, tongue in cheek. "Surely my silence on the matter isn't an out of the way demand. But I would beg a boon, my dear fellow. Please, could you tell me why, since you have been in England for quite some time, you waited until after your brother's funeral to make your existence known to your niece?"

Victoria, who had been standing mute with shock ever since she realized that her Uncle Quentin and Pierre were acquainted, seconded this question, adding hopefully, "But perhaps you hadn't yet come to London at the time the Professor was murdered?"

By this time Sir Perkin, whose hopes of securing more

of the delicious ham had been raised, only to be shot down by Standish's arrival, had decided to take matters into his own hands, and approached the small group to tug on Patrick's sleeve. "I say, Sherbourne," he said brashly, "have you seen that buxomy redhead about lately? Surely you weren't planning on serving only one platter, were you? Though I could push on to Lady Beresford's. Her chef does a fine buffet."

Patrick wasn't in the mood to worry about Sir Perkin's appetite. Pierre, drat the man, had been keeping information from him again, and now it appeared that the Professor's own brother could be a murder suspect. "Run along over there and ask Mrs. Hamilton to help you," he said shortly, disengaging his arm from Seldon's grip. "Just don't smile at her, else Spalding may call you out."

Once the other man had toddled off, already calling plaintively to Emma, Patrick returned his attention to the matter at hand, saying, "Please, Quentin, we're all friends here. Answer Victoria's question."

Quentin took a deep breath, looking at each of them in turn, then said gloomily, "I was in London, all right. I came here directly from Ramsgate."

"Oh, Uncle!" Victoria sighed sadly. "Please, say no more! I don't want to hear any more, really I don't."

Suddenly the crestfallen man became indignant. "Well, I don't know why not, for pity's sake!" he exclaimed hotly. "All I did for nearly a month was kick my heels like some lovestruck lunatic while I waited for my new wardrobe to be finished. I had been in foreign parts for a long time, you know, and didn't want to present myself to Willie until I was fitted out fine as five-pence."

"Perfectly understandable," Pierre put in kindly, sneaking a quick look at Patrick.

"Then you didn't come to see the Professor? But I don't understand. Why didn't you attend the funeral?" Victoria asked, hating herself for needing to know.

"So much for my darling fiancée's declaration that she would be happier to remain in ignorance," Patrick put in, wrapping his arm around her waist. "Don't answer if you don't want to, Quentin. None of us here believes you conked your own brother over the head and then left him to die."

"It wasn't me, because I didn't think of it!" Quentin shot back tightly. "I was here, you know, that same night, only it was earlier in the evening I imagine, as the old bas—, er, m'brother was still very much alive. I'd come to see Willie, of course, but he told me she had moved back to the country to nurse her sick sister. Damn me for a fool, I believed him. By the time I had chased myself to Surrey and back again, Quennel had been carried to bed on six men's shoulders. After that, I didn't see any reason to mention my first visit to anyone. I'm that sorry, you know, if I upset anybody."

"Oh, Uncle," Victoria cried, embracing Quentin, "don't be sorry! *We're* sorry we questioned you. Besides, it's all Mr. Standish's fault for bringing it up in the first place, isn't that right, Patrick?"

The Earl pulled a wry face and looked at his friend, who was standing at his ease, surveying the touching scene unfolding in front of him. "Consider yourself reprimanded, please, dear Pierre, for I refuse to demand retribution. After all, I'm soon to be a married man, and must think of my poor wife and unborn children."

"I offer my apologies, of course, for departing from your prepared script for the evening, my friends," Pierre responded coolly. "I had already assured myself of friend Quinton's innocence, you know. I merely wished to introduce him as a suspect to prove to you all how misleading bits and pieces of seemingly damning evidence can be."

"And how some questions are best left unanswered? Such as an explanation of the contents of a certain wooden box now in your possession?" Victoria, who had grudgingly begun to admire this strange man, questioned incisively.

"Patrick you have unearthed a genuine jewel," Pierre said in a soft, drawling voice. "Guard her well."

CHAPTER TWENTY-TWO

AT THE CONCLUSION of the meal served in the narrow dining room, informal toasts were proposed all round to the happy couple before Wilhelmina (who had steadfastly refused to be one of the party) wheeled in the *pièce de résistance,* a five-tiered cake decorated with meringue swans and bits of greenery that elicited appreciative murmurs from everyone but Sir Perkin, who had immediately leaped to his feet to propose yet another toast—to the cook.

It was while the cake was being served that Patrick looked down the table at Victoria and gave her a barely perceptible nod. Promptly taking her cue, she turned to Philip Spalding, who was seated at her left, and said, "Patrick and I are leaving London within the week to visit his parents—they're spending the season in Bath, you know—to formally announce our engagement, but we wanted to have this small, intimate party here with my uncle in attendance." She then hesitated a moment before adding in a voice heavy with regret, "If only the Professor had been here to give me his blessing."

"Ah, yes," Spalding replied commiseratingly, "it is such a pity, isn't it?"

Victoria sighed deeply. "It seems it was only yesterday that I was sitting in the library, copying down his dictation. Patrick is going to complete the Professor's work, you know, so I believe we can look forward to having the history published in the next year or so.''

''*He isn't!*'' Philip exploded hoarsely, then quickly lowered his voice. ''That is to say, he is? How wonderful. You must be very pleased, Miss Quinton.''

Pierre Standish, seated on the opposite side of the table from Spalding, murmured smoothly, ''Ah, Miss Quinton, well done. A flush hit, I'd say. May I?'' he asked pleasantly, leaning forward slightly to look pointedly at the uncomfortably fidgeting Spalding.

''By all means, Mr. Standish,'' Victoria returned with utmost politeness. ''After all, I believe I owe you at least that much.''

''My dearest Philip,'' Pierre then began urbanely, addressing the patently confused man, ''you seem to be upset about something. Perhaps the cake is too rich for your system—too laden with *cream* for your taste? A pity. I myself have quite a fondness for the stuff. As a matter of fact, I number among my happiest memories those times I would sneak off to the dairy when the servants were making cream. There was one dairymaid I remember in particular—''

Pierre's words were cut off as Spalding, suddenly comprehending, sprang to his feet, knocking over his chair in his haste as he accused dazedly, ''You *know!* How do you know? He promised me no one would know. *He promised!*''

''Obviously there will be no need for the thumbscrews after all,'' Standish said to Victoria, his lips twitching in wry amusement. ''I must admit I am surprised. I truly hadn't thought him to be our man. Perhaps a few more pointed questions are needed?''

''Philip!'' Emma, tugging at his perfectly constructed coat sleeve, cried anxiously, unwittingly casting herself in the role of one of the man's tormentors. "Say it isn't so, *please!* Please say you didn't kill him!"

"Kill him?" Philip repeated hollowly, staring down at Emma, a confused look on his face. "Kill who?"

"Whom," Pierre slid in quietly, clearly enjoying himself.

"Why, the Professor, of course," Emma told him, tears forming in her soft blue eyes as visions of her beloved—dirty, disheveled, and clad in tattered rags as he wallowed in his straw-lined cell—pushed her toward the edge of hysterics. "Was it you who killed the Professor?"

"Arrrgh!"

"Sir Perkin, are you all right?" Quentin asked, pounding the suddenly choking man sharply between the shoulder blades with one beefy fist.

Patrick and Pierre exchanged knowing looks, then turned to Victoria, who surprised them by looking a bit crestfallen rather than triumphant. "We wouldn't publish anything even remotely embarrassing, Mr. Spalding," she told Philip quietly. "Not that having a dairymaid for a great-grandmother is such a terrible thing."

"You know *too?*" Spalding asked, clearly agonized with shame. "The Professor promised me he'd burn his notes. I sold my matched bays to pay him what he—Oh, what difference does it make? Now that Standish knows too—and the rest of you—I imagine everyone will soon be snickering up their sleeves at me. I'll tell you what— I shall have to retire to the country, that's all there is for it, I guess."

"So dramatic, my dear Philip," Pierre drawled sarcastically. "Mrs. Hamilton," he went on, turning to look at Emma, who was crying silently into her handkerchief. "Has the knowledge you have gained in these past few minutes colored your opinion of dear Mr. Spalding here? Come, come. Don't be bashful; a man's future hangs in the balance.''

Bright color suffused Emma's cheeks as she raised her face to peer up at Spalding. "I think he is still the grandest, most noble man that ever lived," she declared at last, before adding thoughtfully, "even if his great-grandmother *was* a Common Nobody."

"You do?" Philip squeaked incredulously. "Don't it even bother you that I was so vain as to pay the Professor not to print that bit about my ancestry?"

"She thinks you hang out the sun, dear boy," Pierre snapped, beginning to lose patience with the ridiculous man. "Don't belabor the point. Now, why don't you escort Mrs. Hamilton to the drawing room—I'm sure you have quite a bit to discuss. Miss Quinton and the rest of us have pressing matters still to resolve."

Offering his hand to Emma, who took it gingerly, Philip helped her to rise, then drew her arm lovingly through his and guided her slowly out of the room, his passionate gaze never leaving her beautiful face. "Was that your maternal or paternal great-grandmother, my dear Mr. Spalding?" Emma was heard to ask pointedly as they walked along.

"Ah, true love," Pierre said emotionlessly once the couple had disappeared through the doors Wilhelmina needed no prompting to close in their wake. "I do not believe there is anything else in this entire mad world that I find so singularly dull and uninteresting."

"And I believe you doth protest too much," Victoria replied bluntly, extremely curious about this enigmatic man who was her fiancé's dearest friend. "Someday I should like to hear the story of how you came to be the cynic you portray so convincingly."

Pierre's dark face suddenly became an emotionless mask, his dark eyes unreadable. "I shall not soil your ears with that sad tale, my dearest Miss Quinton," he snapped coldly, then added more kindly, "Besides, I do believe Sir Perky is about to say something that will interest you. It seems I may have been right all along—though it is tactless in me to remind you, isn't it?"

Indeed, Sir Perkin was recovering from the fit of coughing that had been brought on by Emma's impulsive remarks, wiping at the stream of tears his choking had provoked with Quentin Quinton's immense handkerchief.

Rising to walk to the head of the table, Victoria gratefully sank into the chair Patrick had vacated for her and allowed her hands to be taken in Sir Perkin's compulsive grip.

"He tried to blackmail me too," he began almost incoherently, his lower lip trembling in his agitation.

"Yes, Sir Perky," Victoria assured him kindly, "I know; we all do now, having found certain incriminating papers in the Professor's library. You were not the only victim, I fear, as it appears the man blackmailed a great many people over the years. You just heard Mr. Spalding confess to having paid so that he could keep his own secret safe, didn't you? I can tell you in all honesty, Sir Perky, that Professor Quinton was a vile, soulless man."

"I can't really say I liked him above half myself," Sir Perky admitted, murmuring into his cravat.

"Have another piece of cake, Sir Perkin," Wilhelmina put in, placing a plate holding an immense slice of the dessert in front of the man, hoping he'd then release Victoria's hands. "After all," she said to Patrick as she stepped back to stand beside him, "Missy shouldn't be holdin' hands with a murderer, even if he is the sorriest-looking' fella I've ever seen.''

Wilhelmina's ploy worked, as food had always been a panacea to Sir Perkin, and he quickly shoveled two large bites into his mouth before talking around the resultant bulges in his cheeks. ''The Professor called me to this house to talk about my family history—or so he said. I was flattered to have the Seldons included in his book, of course, and he did serve me the loveliest snack. Duck, I think it was; yes, it was duck. It was only after we had been talking for some time that I realized exactly what he was saying.'' Wiping some cake crumbs from his lips with his serviette, he looked up at Sherbourne and declared earnestly, ''I couldn't believe it of him, I tell you. I just couldn't believe *any* of it!''

''Ah, the treachery of one's friends,'' Patrick commiserated, tongue-in-cheek.''

Sir Perkin held one finger up in the air, signaling that he had something more to say just as soon as he had disposed of the forkful of cake he was at the moment aiming toward his mouth. ''He wasn't my friend,'' he then corrected punctiliously.

''Very well, if you wish to split hairs at a time like this,'' Patrick said amiably. ''Ah, the treachery of one's acquaintances! Is that better? But to continue: The Professor told you about the circumstances of your birth, didn't he?'' Patrick was in a bit of a hurry to get this part of the questioning over, as he could see the tension was beginning to affect Victoria's nerves.

The man nodded his balding head up and down emphatically, licking a bit of meringue from his lips with the tip of his tongue. ''It's not that I minded all that much being a bastard,'' he said in explanation, looking at Victoria for understanding. "It's just that—well—you see, Mama never told me!"

"How remiss of her," Pierre remarked silkily from his seat farther down the table. "Perhaps it slipped her mind."

"Yes!" Sir Perkin exclaimed, jumping on that excuse. "How good of you to see it that way, Mr. Standish. That's precisely what I thought myself, you know, but the Professor had all sorts of papers—church records and the like—that proved I was born before my parents were wed. I was shocked, I tell you," he then told Victoria earnestly, "truly shocked. I mean, everyone says I'm the living spit of my father." His emotional outburst over for the moment, he shoved another forkful of cake between his lips.

"But your father *is* your father," Victoria began hastily, then stopped, looking to Patrick in confusion, for she knew she shouldn't be speaking so freely about such things.

"What Miss Quinton is trying so delicately to say, Sir Perky," Patrick then explained, "is that you *are* your father's son. They were just a trifle tardy with the wedding ceremony, that's all, as christenings don't usually precede the marriage vows. But it was all in the papers the Professor had. Didn't you read them?"

"I—I didn't know." Sir Perkin looked at each of them in turn, swallowed hard, and then asked Wilhelmina if she could please pour him a bit of wine, as his throat was suddenly dry.

"Here you go, Sir Perkin," the housekeeper said bracingly, stepping forward smartly to refill his glass to the rim. "Now don't you go gettin' all upset. Nobody's blamin' you. It was an accident, wasn't it?" she urged, motherlike.

For a moment Victoria feared that Sir Perkin, now looking at the housekeeper like a lost puppy who had just been offered a meaty soup bone, was going to fling himself against Wilhelmina's starched apron and burst into tears, but then he took a deep breath and squared his shoulders, ready to own up to what he had done.

'It was me,'' he said dully at last, shrugging his shoulders. "I did it. I killed him.''

"That's rich, upon my soul it is. Don't plague one with a bag of humbug, does he?'' Quentin remarked happily. "No tippytoeing around the thing, that's for sure. Comes right to the point—bang—'It was me, I killed him.' You have to admire that in a man.''

"Uncle Quentin, please,'' Victoria hissed as Patrick covered his laugh with a discreet cough.

"I never really saw the papers,'' Sir Perkin then informed them, seeming suddenly eager to make a clean breast of everything. "The Professor was just sort of waving them in front of my face, telling me that I was to pay him some ridiculous sum out of my quarterly allowance or else he'd publish the fact that I was a bas—, well, you know that part already. I tried to tell him that I didn't have a feather to fly with—everyone knows that—but he just kept waving those papers back and forth...back and forth...until I swear I couldn't see anything but those papers.''

"Poor little fella,'' Wilhelmina intoned sadly, wiping at her watery eyes with one corner of her apron.

"I guess I must have gone slightly out of my head,'' Sir Perkin then continued in a dull monotone, "for suddenly there was this rather *red* haze in front of my eyes. I lunged for the papers—he held them up and away from me. I grabbed at his arm. We tussled back and forth a bit...with him just laughing and telling me I had to pay...then I somehow lost my grip on him. The Professor fell...hitting his head on the windowsill. It made an awful sound. Then he just sort of slid to the floor...and the papers scattered everywhere. He just lay there, propped against the window, his eyes looking at me but not really seeing anything, if you know what I mean.

"I didn't know what to *do!*" he explained passionately, shaking his head. "I hadn't meant to *hurt* him! He didn't look dead—what with his eyes open and all—and all I could think of was getting myself out of there before he started up and called for help. I closed the drapes over him, I think, and then gathered up my hat and gloves and got out of there as fast as I could."

"Yes," Victoria concurred, reaching into her pocket and extracting the snuffbox to show to him, "but you neglected to gather up more than the papers that concerned you before you left. You also forgot to take this with you. It has your initials on it; that's how we found you. Here," she said kindly, giving him back his property.

"Funny that he missed the snuffbox," Wilhelmina said to no one in particular, "seein' as how he remembered to take up the duck. Weren't any bones in the library when I cleaned it, as I recollect."

"You're going to call for the robin redbreasts now?" Sir Perkin asked Victoria, his chubby face chalky white. "It was an accident, but I still killed him."

"Now here's a dilemma," Pierre mocked, lightly stroking his scarred cheekbone. "I wonder, my dear Miss Quinton, is it a rule of English law that we hang the victim?"

"Don't be facetious, Mr. Standish!" Victoria said hotly, taking one of Sir Perkin's trembling hands in her own. "Although, to be perfectly truthful, I am embarrassed to admit that at first flush I was occupied only with the thrill of the search, and didn't really concern myself as to what I would *do* with the guilty party once I had found him. Indeed, you, Patrick, saw through my motives almost at once," she admitted honestly as her fiancé put a comforting hand on her shoulder.

"But I'm sure I never intended to turn the murderer over to Bow Street—at least not since I discovered what an out and out bounder the Professor really was, which didn't take very long once I was free to search the library at my leisure. Later, once I had uncovered the whole of the Professor's treachery—thanks to help from my Uncle Quentin and Patrick—I knew that it was imperative I continue my search. Oh, not because I was afraid the man might decide he needed to kill me as well to keep his secret safe—as you thought, Patrick, although I allowed you to think that I agreed with your theory."

"Then why, my dearest?" Patrick asked, confused.

Victoria looked up at her beloved, then across the table at the sorry-looking soul who sat quietly awaiting his fate. Squeezing Sir Perkin's fingers reassuringly, she explained, "Why, so that I could apologize to him and assure him that his secret was safe with me, of course."

"*What!*" Patrick exploded, his comforting hand suddenly digging into the tender flesh of her shoulder. "Do you actually mean to sit there and glibly tell me that the only reason you helped us arrange this whole scheme was so that we could unmask Sir Perkin—in order that you might be able to *apologize to him?* That it has nearly always been your intention to apologize to the Professor's murderer—even before you allowed Quentin and me to help you? I don't believe it! You romantic idiot! Didn't you realize somewhere in your silly, romantic head that the murderer could have killed *you* as well when you gifted him with your polite apology—just in case you might someday have had second thoughts in the matter?''

''Mr. Standish could have killed me,'' Victoria corrected, quite calmly explaining her logic, ''not that I would have considered going on with my plan if I discovered that *he* was the murderer. I'm not *that* much of a zany. Sir Perkin is much more understanding.''

''I don't believe any of this,'' Patrick grumbled, subsiding heavily into a chair beside his softly chuckling friend.

''I make no doubt, darling Patrick, that you'll be graying within the year,'' Pierre drawled, reaching for his wineglass. ''Marriage has that effect on your gender, I'm told.''

Victoria refused to apologize for doing what she felt in her heart to be right. ''I don't understand what all the fuss is about,'' she argued indignantly. ''Even though investigating the murder seemed to be a golden opportunity for me to enjoy myself a little bit before hiring myself out as a governess or some such thing, from the very beginning I had a feeling that something was very, very wrong. As he lay dying, the Professor had kept impressing upon me the fact that I had to make his murderer 'pay.' At first I thought he meant the murderer should pay for his crime, but it soon became apparent to me that he had another sort of payment in mind entirely. Contrary to what I allowed you to believe, Patrick, I had discovered the Professor's private ledger and examined it long before you urged Uncle Quentin to show it to me. I had already known about the Professor's blackmailing activities for some time.''

Patrick tried to say something, only to be cut off by

the love of his life as she continued matter-of-factly, "It was then that I stopped searching for the murderer out of some ridiculous loyalty to the Professor and pushed on for quite another reason entirely—to ease the poor murderer's conscience for having acted, under great distress I was sure, to remove a threat to his security. After all, I *too* had been living on the money the Professor was extorting from all those poor souls, although I didn't know it."

Sherbourne, his voice sounding strangely strained, muttered something that could have been "windmills," before slapping his forehead with his palm and exploding vehemently, "Of all the imbecilic, asinine, *quixotic*—"

Standish, who had risen languidly to his feet shut off the tirade with a warning shake of his head. "Let it go, dear boy," Pierre advised sagely. "Understanding the workings of a woman's mind is a lifelong study. You shan't be able to fathom such intricacies in one short evening. Now, if I might suggest you return your attentions to poor Sir Perky here, who is still looking a bit stunned by your fiancée's gracious forgiveness? Perhaps another slice of that delicious cake?"

Sir Perkin, who was feeling quite mellow, actually, now that he knew he wasn't about to be carted off to the guardhouse, rubbed his rounded stomach reflectively, saying, "Oh no, no, no! I couldn't eat another bite."

"I've got some cherry tarts in the kitchen left from luncheon," Wilhelmina suggested, having developed a real fondness for the chubby little man.

"You do?" Sir Perkin exclaimed, already rising to his feet. "You know, when I was just a lad in Wiltshire our cook would let me sit in her kitchen and watch her while she baked cherry tarts. I was always happy in the kitchens, what with all those wonderful smells and those lovely bowls to lick. I say, do you suppose…?''

Wilhelmina slipped an arm around Sir Perkin's shoulders and gave him a slight push toward the baize-covered door that led to the servants' portion of the house. ''Done and done! You come with me and Quentin, Sir Perky,'' she said bracingly, ''and you can watch me whilst I roll out a whole fresh batch. Right, Quentin?''

''Right you are, love,'' Quentin agreed, going ahead of them to open the door that led down a narrow hallway to the kitchen. ''I could do with one of your cherry tarts m'self.''

''And as the stage grows dim, the players drift away into the shadows, their stories told, their happiness assured.'' So saying, Pierre Standish made to move toward the hallway, adding, ''I bid you good evening, my friends. It has been utterly delightful, I assure you—better than anything I have seen at Covent Garden in many a season—but a wise man knows when he has become dreadfully in the way. Isn't that correct, my dearest Patrick?''

Sherbourne, now standing before Victoria, his hands resting lightly on her shoulders as he gazed adoringly into her eyes, didn't bother to reply, knowing that Pierre had already slipped silently out of the room.

''I like him, you know,'' Victoria said of Standish as she reached her arms up and around Patrick's neck. ''I know he's dangerous and secretive and all those other things, but I really do like him.''

''I should box your ears,'' Patrick replied quietly, trying to look stern and failing badly in the effort. ''You do know that, don't you? Why didn't you tell me what you planned to do when Sir Perkin confessed?''

"Do you know something, my dearest, most darling Patrick? You ask too many questions," Victoria replied sweetly, moving her lips to within a heartbeat of his— and effectively putting an end to their conversation.

EPILOGUE

"PERHAPS WE CAN TELL HIM we're keeping it for our oldest son to present to his wife," Victoria, trying to be helpful, suggested, holding the ornate diamond-encrusted brooch in front of her and looking at it assessingly.

"A brooch in the shape of a Q as a betrothal gift?" her husband quipped in amused disbelief. "At least it would be a true test of her devotion. After all, if the poor girl didn't really love our offspring, she'd run screaming posthaste for her papa to send a retraction to the newspapers, wouldn't she?"

Victoria giggled happily at the joke and then leaned back against Patrick's broad chest. "It is atrocious, isn't it? Dear Uncle Quentin, he means well."

"Wilhelmina was ecstatic about the necklace he gave her as a wedding token," the Earl said, his voice deliberately bland. "But then, of course, Willie does have a magnificent bosom, just the sort for showing such a heavy piece off to good advantage."

"Wretch!" Victoria shot back, poking him in the ribs with her elbow. Then, sobering slightly, she went on, "They're only gone a week and I miss them already. While neither may be related to me by blood, they're the only family—besides you, dearest, and the children we shall share—that I could ever want. Do you miss them too?"

Patrick leaned down to plant a soft kiss on the top of her head. "Yes, love, I do—and we are not the only ones. I hear Sir Perky has all but gone into mourning, now that his supply of tarts has been cut off. But they'll be happier in Surrey, love. Wilhelmina had no craving for London, even if Quentin's money could buy them a limited place in Society. And we'll visit them often, I promise. Just be glad Emma and Philip have at last set the date. I was beginning to think we had taken on a full-time boarder."

"Emma or Philip?" Victoria teased, looking out over the softly rolling hills of Sherbourne's country estate. "He certainly did make a pest of himself, didn't he, nearly drowning poor Emma with that constant shower of gifts he brought round to our town house almost daily. Honestly, to think he could actually believe dear, sweet Emma would consider him beneath her touch after finding out about his great-grandmother. I thought she'd have to compromise the silly man in order for him to believe she really did wish to become Mrs. Spalding."

Shifting his weight slightly on the blanket they had spread out beneath one of the apple trees on the fringe of the orchard, Patrick reached his arms more fully around his wife and gave her slim waist a gentle squeeze. "Truth to tell, pet, I do think she was slightly taken aback for a while, before she considered all of her options. She made her point rather well at the end, I think, asking Spalding if he truly believed she wished to spend the rest of her life carrying around the name Emma Hamilton. All in all, I'd say the two of them were made for each other."

"You would?" Victoria asked, twisting her head around to look up at him.

"Not really," he answered in all honesty, "but it was

either that or having the two of them underfoot indefinitely.''

''Oh you—'' she exclaimed in feigned exasperation, rolling over to pin him against the blanket. ''Sometimes you are as maddeningly sarcastic as your friend Pierre Standish!''

''I kiss better than Pierre Standish, *darling,*'' Patrick declared, grinning up at her.

''You do?''

''Of course I do. Come here, minx, and I'll prove it.''

''But however shall I know if you are telling the truth, having never kissed Pierre Standish?'' Victoria asked, lifting a hand to remove her spectacles and lay them beside her on the blanket. ''Perhaps you should write to Mr. Standish in London and apply to him for assistance in proving your point?''

''Pierre's not in London, pet,'' her husband informed her, slipping a hand behind her neck and slowly pulling her down to him. ''He's been called to his father's estate in the country. It's strange, but I don't think he's been to visit his father since we first returned from the Peninsula to find his mother had died during his absence.''

''I didn't know his father was still living. As a matter of fact, it never occurred to me that one such as Pierre ever *had* a father—yet alone a mother.''

''Spawn of the devil, you mean,'' Patrick said, nuzzling her throat where it rose above the collar of her gown. ''And to think that the poor fellow likes you.''

Victoria pulled away slightly to protest. ''I like him *too*. I just don't *understand* him, that's all. There are too many questions about him—too many questions and very few answers. Do you think we will ever learn just what is contained in that infernal wooden box? Or why he has changed so much since his return from the war?''

"Maybe we wouldn't like the answers," Patrick suggested thoughtfully, a small frown creasing the skin between his eyebrows. "Besides," he said, brightening, "I have already found all *my* answers—in you. Come here, my dearest wife, and tell me again: Who is your dearest, dearest love?"

"You are, of course." Victoria sighed on a smile, before settling her lips on his and surrendering to his embrace.

A long, lovely time later Patrick whispered into her ear, "Any more questions, my darling Victoria?"

His delighted wife only smiled.

HARLEQUIN *Super* ROMANCE®

...there's more to the story!

Superromance.
A *big* satisfying read about unforgettable
characters. Each month we offer *six* very different
stories that range from family drama to adventure
and mystery, from highly emotional stories to
romantic comedies—and much more! Stories
about people you'll believe in and care about.
Stories too compelling to put down....

Our authors are among today's *best* romance
writers. You'll find familiar names and talented
newcomers. Many of them are award winners—
and you'll see why!

If you want the biggest and best
in romance fiction, you'll get it
from Superromance!

Emotional, Exciting, Unexpected...

HARLEQUIN®
Makes any time special ®

HARLEQUIN *Presents*

**The world's bestselling romance series...
The series that brings you your favorite authors,
month after month:**

Helen Bianchin...Emma Darcy
Lynne Graham...Penny Jordan
Miranda Lee...Sandra Marton
Anne Mather...Carole Mortimer
Susan Napier...Michelle Reid

and many more uniquely talented authors!

Wealthy, powerful, gorgeous men...
Women who have feelings just like your own...
The stories you love, set in exotic, glamorous locations...

HARLEQUIN *Presents*

Seduction and passion guaranteed!

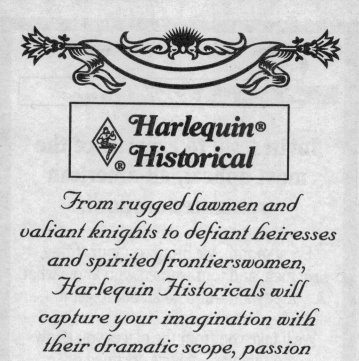

Harlequin® Historical

From rugged lawmen and valiant knights to defiant heiresses and spirited frontierswomen, Harlequin Historicals will capture your imagination with their dramatic scope, passion and adventure.

*Harlequin Historicals...
they're too good to miss!*